# Pellucid Lunacy

### Edited by Michael Bailey

# Pellucid Lunacy

# Contents

"A soul that makes virtue its companion is like an overflowing well, for it is clean and pellucid, sweet and wholesome, open to all, rich, blameless and indestructible."

– Epictetus


"What can you do against the lunatic who is more intelligent than yourself, who gives your arguments a fair hearing and then simply persists in his lunacy?"

– George Orwell

# The Other Side of the Glass

## Rick McQuiston

The memories of the previous day slid into Peter's weary mind and settled like uninvited dinner guests. If he could go back in time, he never would have left the house that day, opting instead to spend it shut away from the strange, greasy film on his windows and the leering glare from his mirrored self.

"You can't hide from me, you know," the other Peter drawled through the glass.

Peter shivered. Even though his features were the same, the eyes were colder, distant—eyes that reveled in the misery and destruction of others.

"It's too late for you now," the other Peter said. "You crossed the threshold. You took the preverbal plunge, if you will."

"It wasn't my fault. I didn't ask to see it. I didn't know."

"That may very well be true, but it changes nothing. I don't make the rules. I dwell with many others in the nether regions between belief and disbelief, between reality and unreality, between sanity and insanity."

Peter's stomach tightened.

"Others?"

The other Peter laughed. "So many, you wouldn't believe it."

"I didn't ask for this. I—"

"Of course not."

Peter's imitation smiled wider, the mouth nearly splitting his head in two. He expected the top portion of it to slide off and slop to the ground. He tilted his head to one side and said, "There are far worse things lurking in unreality. Once the line is crossed, there's no going back. Perspective changes. Boundaries distort to levels dreamt in the minds of madmen."

He was helpless. How could he, or anyone, fight such things? Peter looked to the floor, his mouth tightening into a grimace, fists clenching.

The other Peter was distorted by the translucent film behind the glass.

"Your world is different now. You might as well accept it."

Peter reached for the phone, but it dissolved into slime before he could grab it.

"There's no going back. You saw something you

should not have seen … something that doesn't exist, but *does* exist. And from that moment on, everything you knew is different now, as I'm sure you have noticed for yourself."

Peter ran into the kitchen, yanking open drawers and cabinets to find a weapon. Arming himself seemed paramount, yet his hopes were quickly deflated. Everything he sought after morphed into something terrible: a stainless-steel butcher knife transformed into a hissing serpent; a tray of cutlery changed into a writhing mass of hairy spiders; a broomstick sprouted glossy black wings and talons too numerous to count.

"Do you believe me now?"

Peter fell onto his couch. Sweat trickled his face as his heart raced. He knew he had no other choice but to believe.

"That's right. You don't have a choice. Our kind so rarely has any chances to reveal ourselves to your world. You see, Peter, there are a great many things that exist in the realm of impossibility, most of which are never seen by people in the real world. Occasionally, one as unfortunate as yourself—or lucky, depending on the disposition—crosses the threshold."

"It wasn't my fault. I was taking pictures of the beach. Something came out of the water. It flooded my lens. It was red … no, blue. So many heads. So many teeth."

The other Peter laughed. "You sound like you're losing your mind already. But not to worry."

"What do you mean?"

"I'm afraid I neglected to tell you something important. You see, the real world—your world—is still here. Its existence has not been diluted nor erased. The borders still apply."

"So I'm safe?"

"I'm afraid so. However, you retain the knowledge of what you saw. Of course, you will attempt to deny it as time goes by, perhaps even seek therapy, but that will change little because the irreplaceable fact that you did see it will remain. Our world continually chips away at yours. Eventually, everyone will believe enough to crumble the barrier completely, and then …"

"I don't care. Leave me alone. I didn't see anything. This door is closed. Do you hear me? Closed!"

The other Peter smiled. He raised his hands and pushed his palms together. He inched them forward as if parting a set of curtains, and sliced through the greasy film outside the window. Mottled fingertips tapped against the glass.

"The barrier will crumble when enough people believe." A dark glint crossed his face. "Like it or not, *you* believe."

"You said I was safe."

"I did, and at the time I meant it. But that was then and this is now. Things change, even out here."

The other Peter tapped on the glass a little harder. Chipped fingernails etched the glass. Translucent slime dripped from the face of the window and pooled on the sill. An acrid stench slipped into the room.

Peter felt his sanity slipping away like water through a crack, his head sagging to his chest. His eyes fluttered as a slow descent into madness settled over him.

"And now, since you believe, I welcome you to my world."

The wall sheared away at that moment, flying into the gloom-shrouded beyond and plunging into oblivion.

A cold breeze washed over him and with it the stench of stagnant water and decay.

"You may as well look. A man at least deserves to see his fate."

The smells were familiar: damp sand, cool air tinged with a fishy aroma, stagnant brine drifting from the sea. A soggy stench.

Peter lifted his head.

The wide grin on the other Peter's face looked painful. The strange, greasy film was dripping off his body, as if he had been swimming in the stuff.

"There's someone here who wants to meet you."

Peter's remaining strength dribbled away, and with it fell the last shreds of his sanity.

"It remembers you from that day on the beach. And you were correct on both counts. It is both red and blue, a rather unique combination of the two shades. I doubt there's anything like it in your world."

An enormous, malformed head rose from

behind the other Peter. Its eyes were the size of dinner plates, its gaping maw littered with countless teeth. It lifted its foul head twenty feet in the air before shaking violently from side to side, as if trying to rid the greasy film covering its body. And then it locked its terrible gaze on Peter and reared, preparing to strike.

# Here You Come Again

## Julian Cantella

The children weren't perfect copies, not exactly. They weren't doppelgangers either, nor mirrored images of Jolene's adult body shrunken to the size of toddlers or grade-schoolers or even teenagers. The children looked as if they had been ripped from her womb, taking something essential of hers along with them.

She'd pass them on the side of the road and see their grass-stained jeans and faces brown with dust. She'd see them at the playground, stopped at the bottom of the slide. They knew. At night the wind carried their voices through her bedroom window.

*We're going to die. What you gave us is broken.*

They didn't entirely belong to her. There was always that other half, the part that came from someone else: an aloof posture, green iris, angular nose. Enough to suggest another person had played a part in their creation.

Her children were everywhere.

To avoid them, Jolene wanted to bolt the doors of her home, paint the windows black and let the air in her bedroom turn warm and moist. She'd feel buried beneath the earth, or as if she were inside her mother's womb, waiting.

A little boy took her hand as she stepped onto an escalator one day. She knew it was hers. And then a crack appeared in his forehead. It was small at first, but quickly widened. Blood as thick as syrup spilled over his eyes, crawled over his cheek and dribbled from his chin, finally pooling at his feet.

Jolene screamed, jerking her hand away.

The boy erupted in tears, his body wracked by sobs even as his face split and fell away to reveal a pale skull beneath.

A woman was waiting at the top of the escalator. Her eyes were cold as she scooped the child into her arms. She softly patted his back and hurried to the nearest exit.

Someone nudged Jolene from behind. She took her eyes off the boy for a moment, but could feel the words he whispered.

"We're everywhere, Mommy. All your murdered children."

Jolene bought a long mirror so she could study herself. After her husband left for work, she'd strip away her clothes, lay them on the bedspread and confront her reflection. She recognized the strange fold at the top of her right ear; it belonged to a little girl she'd seen at church. A baby at the supermarket had displayed the dark crescents that drooped from her eyes. At the movie theater, the girl at the concession stand had kicked her left foot out like Jolene when she turned to fill a bag of popcorn.

She tried to point it out to her husband, but he never noticed.

When she was able to have children, Jolene gave birth to Alex and Tammy. Eighteen months apart, they did everything together, tore through the house in a whirlwind of uniforms and lunch boxes and schoolbooks. Jolene was happily swept up in it as years of her life passed by in a blur of science projects and soccer games and play dates and parties.

"I know you say I spread myself too thin," she told her husband, hoping to disarm him with humor, "but I can't imagine wanting something so bad and having your body say no. I want to share what I have … if anyone will have me."

"Your body," he replied, unable to conceal his surprise, "your call."

Jolene researched the process and conducted informational visits with local clinics. They walked her through each step, test, and confidentiality agreement, wrote quotes for compensation with red felt-tip pens.

"They're worth that? I have thousands." Then, smiling: "How much for the rest of me?"

She settled on a firm called Community Surrogates, a relatively small operation located in an unassuming brick building a few miles down the highway. Her husband found them blunt. As long as they were safe and honest, Jolene reasoned, nothing else mattered.

The tests were stressful. Jolene hadn't anticipated the hesitation she felt when it came time to give up her rights.

"Any regret, best to back out now," said the nurse. "When you sign, they belong to someone else."

Jolene surprised herself by snatching the pen from the nurse.

"They'll always be mine."

She injected the hormones, her body going into periods of controlled hyper-stimulation that resulted in multi-egg production during cycles. If she'd conceived, she might have found herself pregnant with three or four embryos, maybe more. But she was careful, and when it was time for the removal surgery, she passed all blood tests and pelvic exams.

The surgery began with an ultrasound. Jolene watched the needle on the screen as it navigated to her ovaries. It was a quick procedure—no more than twenty-five minutes—and since she was under light anesthesia, she was able to trace the path of the follicles as they left her body one by one. She found it beautiful and was enthralled that she could experience the joy and wonder of giving birth while keeping her head clear enough to appreciate it.

A few months later, she did it a second time.

Spring brought round number three, with the fourth not much later.

"Here you come again," she said, trying to individualize the eggs in her mind. Each egg—a piece of her body no larger than a pinhead—might in time become a child whose face, whose voice, whose fingers and thoughts would reflect a part of herself.

Jolene struggled to replay those memories. The images were blurry and filled with static. How many eggs, how many children? Fifty? A hundred?

However many there were, she was responsible for all of them.

And they were waiting for her.

She pictured them gathering on her lawn: the toddlers holding hands, barely able to keep upright; others with their feet planted at shoulder-width, wielding paring knives or garden trowels.

"Here you come again," she'd say, giving them tacit permission to exact their revenge.

As they set upon her—the older ones methodically taking turns, the toddlers slapping hands and singing, "Here you go! Here you go!" over and over—Jolene never once raised a hand in self-defense. Instead, as she sank to the ground, she'd try to capture their faces in her mind. She had to make it up to them somehow. If they wanted her life, well, that might be a start.

"Here I go," she'd say, suddenly alone.

Jolene drove to Community Surrogates one day and asked to see her records.

"Ma'am, you know better. We can give you copies of your agreement and test results, but that's it. I know you have those already, so I'm going to take this call."

The blunt mannerisms Jolene used to appreciate had long since lost their charm.

"I have new information," she said, absentmindedly drawing on the sign-in sheet. "It's extremely important."

The nurse answered the phone, tugged the sign-in sheet from Jolene's grasp, and closed the reception window.

"We have it already," she said, cupping a calloused hand over the receiver. "It's all been dealt with."

A procession of action figures marched around the perimeter of the nurse's desk. Pressed against the window, Jolene tried identifying the characters to see if she could picture any of them in the hands of Tammy or Alex, but they all looked the same. The nurse pecked a few keys on the keyboard as her voice droned idly. When the call ended, the window slid open.

"How many?" Jolene asked, her fingers crawling across the counter. "How many have died?"

The nurse poked her head through the window and whispered, "It's a tragedy, no doubt. Whatever happens, it's over and done. There's nothing we can do, not now."

The doctors described it as an early-onset version of *retinal vasculopathy* with *cerebral leukodystrophy*. RVCL, for short. They had never seen it in children before, nor seen it progress so quickly. It hit Tammy first, but by the time she began suffering from dementia, Alex was already losing his sight.

With her husband at work, it was Jolene using the flash cards trying to stave off memory loss, Jolene cushioning the children's heads and draining fluid from their mouths when they lapsed into seizures, Jolene keeping the paths through the house clear when they went blind, and Jolene's voice they heard through the mist of pain and confusion.

Within two years, they were both gone, buried side-by-side in the family plot.

Jolene considered her other children.

Doctors led her into a conference room where they confirmed the worst. RVCL was genetic. It was easily inherited, but not so easily detected. They had tested Jolene for everything when she shared her eggs with the world, but they didn't know about the new RVCL. No one did.

By the time Jolene told Community Surrogates about the poison hidden in her body, five years had passed since the first donation. Five years for her eggs to spread the disease, fill wombs and take seed and spring forth as flowers destined to wilt and die long before they could ever hope to blossom.

"The gene won't always express itself," one of the doctors said, as if there was comfort in uncertainty. "It may lie dormant for a time, or remain latent for an entire childhood. You survived."

Of course Jolene had survived; she was a carrier. She had lived long enough to pass it on.

Sometimes the children ignored Jolene, but she still heard their voices:

*She thought her body was clean.*

*But when she found out …*

*She only thought of the ones she could keep, the ones who were hers.*

*And us?*

*We weren't whole, not yet.*

*Maybe that's why she waited so long, to let more of us spill from her body so we could taste a bit of air before dying.*

Opening her eyes, Jolene found herself on a beach.

There were hundreds of people: men beating the sand from their towels, women shading their eyes with the crook of their arms, children running from the incoming tide. Jolene felt alone for the first time in a long while. Despite the sun warming her belly, the salt flecking her tongue, the chatter of gulls and distant conversations, her mind was empty.

Scanning the crowd, Jolene felt a sudden burst of panic. "Where …" She tried to rouse her husband, but he wasn't there.

"Where are my children?"

She rose to her feet, slipped on a pair of thongs and jogged to the shore. The thin foam of a wave rushed to meet her. "Where ... where?" she muttered, gaining speed as she skirted the border that separated dry sand from wet.

Jolene searched for the telltale signs of her daughter: a fold at the top of a girl's right ear, dark crescents beneath an infant's eyes, a teenager kicking her left foot out as she reached for a Frisbee. She listened for Alex, for the high-pitched giggle that would burst free when he was too excited to hold it back; it always made his face red with embarrassment. She rifled through rumpled towels to find one with a winking moon; it was Tammy's favorite, always coming untied and sliding down her thin legs when she ran. She looked for children with her spindly arms, short stubby fingers, children who had never truly left her side, not since the day she first realized her condition.

Twenty minutes passed, and then an hour. The tide receded, the sun fading behind a mass of low-hanging clouds.

A lifeguard tapped Jolene on the shoulder. "If you're worried about your children, we can call the beach patrol. Have you checked the condo? Maybe they're by the pool, or ..."

Jolene wasn't listening. Among all the children on the beach, she had failed to find a familiar face.

"I'm sorry, I forgot. They were never here."

They were all dead. Not just Alex and Tammy. All of them.

At around two in the morning, Jolene drove to Community Surrogates. She wrapped her hand within a beach towel—displaying the winking moon—and broke the window. After fiddling with the lock, she let herself in through the door.

An alarm sounded, shrill and persistent. She'd only have a few minutes.

The first group of children waited patiently in the reception area: two boys and a girl. They played with a toy propped between piles of magazines, moving colored wooden blocks along a series of undulating wires. Jolene watched as blocks collided.

The children laughed until they noticed Jolene, and then they stopped playing.

*I was eight*, the girl said, playing with her hands.

*I was six*, one of the boys said.

The third child lurched forward, unsteady on his feet. He was falling apart, ankles snapping under the weight of his body, fluids draining to the floor, skin sloughing away from bone.

*Mommy?* He didn't wait for a response. *I was three.*

Jolene ran blindly through hallways choked with children, all hers.

Some called after her, or reached for her hands or scratched her legs as she passed. Jolene ducked into an office and saw a forest of children with empty, unrecognizing eyes. They held out stiff arms and spoke nonsense from mouths hanging open like doors with broken hinges. A procedure room overflowed with children locked in spasm, the slap of their limbs on the walls reverberating over and over, the din so loud Jolene thought the room would collapse.

Through hallways and shadows and seemingly endless rooms of children, she finally found Alex and Tammy.

They pointed to a door.

*Look in there.*

She thought she'd found the records, but the soft blue glow of the room radiating cold spoke of something else.

Stainless steel freezers hugged three long walls, and there was a central counter lined with chemicals and inscrutable collections of equipment. Jolene took a slow tour of the room, her palms held out to absorb the chill. On the second lap, she knew exactly where to stop.

The container was smaller than a pillbox, the eggs within like dots from a ballpoint pen. She counted them, taking time to give thanks for all twelve.

They would never be born, and would never have to die.

Jolene looked up from the eggs to find the room filled with her children—those who had been born with the poison and died.

She recognized the boy from the department store and the girl from the concession stand. Others carried trowels or bore faces flecked with

Jolene's blood. The children filled every corner of the room, standing arm to arm and cheek to cheek, pressed against the walls and crouching under the counter and spilling out into the hallways and reception area and parking lot. She knew they lined the streets to Jolene's house, where they sat on her stoop and ate at her table and shivered under the covers of her bed.

Closest to Jolene were Tammy and Alex.

*Mommy …*

They were smiling, but there was no joy.

*We're all here now. All in line so you can see who you killed.*

Jolene tried to step away, but there was nowhere to go. The freezer was cold against her back.

"I didn't know," she said. "I would do anything to change this."

Her two children—the first to gain life and first to die—reached out, each placing a hand at a point below Jolene's stomach.

*There's nothing wrong here.*

*You can bring us back.*

"How?"

Jolene already knew the answer.

Alex handed her a needle.

Tammy handed her the first container of eggs.

The eggs within were not hers and were not infected; they could make life that could last. Every child held a container.

*Bring us back*, they said as one. *We'll come again.*

Somewhere in the distance a new alarm sounded,

more urgent, but Jolene had plenty of time.

She readied the needle and imagined herself giving birth to hundreds of children all at once. Giving her life to bring them all back.

"Here I go," she said, closing her eyes.

# Locked Up

### Kia Storm

I'm at an audition of some kind. Somehow I must have lost my days again. It happens. I wake and find that a day or even a week has passed. I'm alive because I escaped.

I explained to my friends that three men in jackets had kidnapped me, but neither Corey nor Jeff believed me. They never did.

"You're a liar," Corey said, brushing back her hair. "You always think someone is trying to kill you." Jeff didn't say anything, but he smirked at Corey.

I hate when their whispers hush to silence whenever I walk into the room. I hate their laughter even more.

"Next," a receptionist calls out.

*Don't panic. You can do this.*

I rise from my chair. My heart beats so fast that

I'm sure the woman sitting next to me is humming to the sound of it.

"Stop doing that," I tell her.

Her demeanour turns evil through her tinted glasses. She mutters the word psycho and returns to her magazine.

*No one knows*, I remind myself.

The receptionist points at two men who motion me to follow. A door creaks and I reluctantly enter before it slams shut, locking me inside. The room is solid black. I shake the knob and slam my fists against the door.

"Shh C"

A tiny glow. The two men from before grin, their faces shiny. Sudden blasts of light brighten the room. There are three chairs and a desk and they gesture for me to sit.

The thin one with the receding hairline stands directly in front of me. A tape recorder drones on the desk. He puts his hand on my shoulder, stopping me from rocking in my seat.

"Where did you hide them?"

"I don't know what you're talking about. Is this … is this the audition?"

The larger one puts his fist in front of my face and says, "Why did you do it?"

"Do what?"

The thin one throws a chair at me, but I duck under the table and go for the door.

"Let me out!" I tell them. "Someone, please help me!"

I sink in quicksand. Tiny hands crawl up my legs, pulling at me.

*What's happening?*

Fingers dig into my skin.

*I don't want to die.*

"She'll be fine," says a comforting voice.

Shadowy figures hover over me. A woman strokes my forehead, but she's merely a silhouette.

"Mom, is that you?"

"You're hallucinating. This is a side effect."

As my vision clears, I see the thin man with the receding hairline. I am still in that tiny room, but there is no laughter and hands no longer bind me. The receptionist points to a chair at a table across from him.

The woman with the magazine is still next to me.

"So you did it?" the man presses. "Your fingerprints are all over the house. Where are the bodies?"

There is no one to trust. Not my doctors. Not my mother. No one can save me. I cover my ears and hum … anything to erase the scene, the voices and the confusion.

*Go away! I can't hear you. There is no waiting room … no woman … no mother … no laughter. You're all in my mind. I didn't do it!*

I struggle to wake myself.

"Next."

The woman with the dark tinted glasses looks up from her magazine. "I think it's my turn." She smiles unexpectedly. "Good luck."

I nod, but I can't find solace, not even in the people who show me kindness. I scan the room. Near trance of the waiting area the receptionist laughs with a beautiful blonde girl. The pretty girls, always belittling me.

"You okay?" The woman next to me whispers, "You need to freshen up. You can't go in there like that. It's going to be fine. Don't worry. You're hallucinating. It's a side effect. It will be over before you know it."

The receptionist asks me to follow her into a large room. After trudging in I say, "Please don't close the door. Please don't—"

She locks me in anyway.

A coffin faces me.

I pound on the door until my knuckles bleed and I can no longer feel them. A screech and the coffin lid opens, filling the room with a hideous stench. I cover my mouth and nose, but I kneel on the floor and vomit.

A man rises out of the coffin and moves toward me.

I spider-crawl until backed against the wall.

I try to close my eyes, but can't.

Jeff stands near me with blood and teeth marks covering his skin. He coughs a watery mixture of blood and it splashes over my face, into my mouth.

I spit, yet something sticks in my throat, a taste of salt and skin.

Jeff smirks over his shoulder to the coffin. Corey climbs out next and ambles forward.

*None of this is real.*

"Next."

I stand on the theatre stage in front of a panel. Time has fallen away from me again.

"What's your piece?"

*It's an audition.*

I breathe out slowly and say, "A monologue."

"By whom?"

I pause, unable to answer.

"Okay then, when you're ready."

I clear my throat.

"There were three of us by the pool and I was afraid of the water. Jeff laughed and Corey laughed, too. At this point, they had lost faith in everything I had said. *You're going crazy*, they told me. *We should let your mother know.* I think it was Corey who said this; she could be so cruel. *Off your medication much? You're going all psycho again, aren't you?*

"They never took me seriously. They were always laughing. I can still see it in their eyes. They wanted me to go to that place and rot. I will never go there again.

"We were staying in a villa for two weeks. It was Corey's idea to bring Jeff. She knew her parents wouldn't let her go away with a guy. She's pretty and popular and I didn't mind people using me for a cover. Until they sent me to that congested room. It was tiny, like a box. They told me to give them privacy. *Do us a little favor*, Corey said.

"The more I sat, alone, the angrier I became, and then I heard it … that voice: *Everything will be better for you if they are gone. You can't go to that horrible place.*

"I snuck into the kitchen and rummaged through the drawers for some sort of protection. The hours snuck away from me, and Jeff was nowhere to be found. Corey was intoxicated and passed out in her room. Even though her eyes were closed, I heard her giggling.

*You okay?* Corey whispered, half-asleep.

I reached into the pocket of my dress and pulled out the butcher knife I found in the kitchen.

"She looked so peaceful, so beautiful. The voice in my head told me to do it. I raised the knife. I stabbed her a few times, and then a few more to make sure she was dead. I dragged her body to the pool and pushed her in.

"That's when Jeff stumbled, drunk. He had puke on his shirt. I told him Corey was drowning and he rushed to the water. The voice in my head returned … it told me to grab one of the free weights at my feet. He jumped in and carried her body to the edge of the pool. I hit him hard over the head, twice, and he let go of Corey's body. The pool water clouded with their blood, and the way Jeff was struggling and slipping and sinking and finally gone …

"It was beautiful."

"Stop," someone from the audience shouted.

But I didn't stop.

"It took me a long time to figure out what to do with the bodies. I waited for the night and then I dragged them both into the woods. It took all night. I didn't clean the house in the villa for a while. We had it reserved for two weeks."

"Your story is interesting, but this isn't a monologue."

"It is real!" I shouted. "It's very real!"

I feel the drugs wearing thin. I open my eyes and attempt to get out of bed, but I can't and I fall. I am still locked away in the room. Corey and Jeff stand at my side. The door opens and two policemen approach. One is thin and balding and the other is plump.

"The doctors say you need to keep taking your meds or they'll have to keep sedating you. The sooner you realize that Brentwood Asylum is your home, the better."

"They are beside me."

"What did you say?" asked the thin one, pulling on his gaunt cheeks.

"They won't leave me alone."

I giggled uncontrollably, pointing to Corey and Jeff.

# What the Walrus Hears

### Jim Ehmann

In her head, Kara screamed. She fled her office at the university and walked briskly to her bus stop. The union-protected baboons in the next cubicle, giggling and howling all day, had taken their toll on her mood. She could handle managing tens of millions of dollars in research funds, but not the junior-high-school-lunch-room atmosphere. The irony of escaping the prestigious university to seek intelligent life depressed her further.

There was one more annoyance to endure, she knew. The Walrus was there, waiting for the bus. Somehow he reminded Kara of a cartoon animal, a vague memory from her television childhood. He was in full Walrus uniform: sandals, Levis flipped at the ankles, faded Hawaiian shirt, a ridiculous comb-over, drooping mustache, extensive gut bulging over a wide belt. Always the same.

The aggravating part was the Walrus' ritual performance on the bus. Once seated, he would put on the headphones and pull out a book. Within seconds, his head would nod steadily. Then the top of the head would wag, a smirk spreading across his face, toes tapping. Soon he'd close his eyes and abandon the book, lost in reverie. Then he'd cut loose, the walrus head thrusting emphatically, body swaying in his seat. His wide grin—idiotic and grating to Kara—spoke of pure, mindless joy.

After witnessing many repetitions of this routine, Kara began speculating about the music fueling the performance. The Walrus appeared to be in his late fifties, which meant he would have been collegeaged during the late sixties or early seventies. He could have been a hippie, but his body language did not suggest psychedelic noodling or blistering electric guitars. She concluded it must be something simple, mindless. The Beach Boys, perhaps.

Kara followed the Walrus onto the bus and her mind unfortunately retrieved a memory of The Archies singing "Sugar Sugar." She dreaded how long it would take to get it out of her head.

The side bench near the back offered the only empty seat ... next to the Walrus. Kara edged into the narrow space. She had never heard his voice; however, while waiting at the bus stop, she often perceived he was inspecting her. That was not so unusual; Kara's myriad tattoos drew plenty of attention. Still, he made her uncomfortable, and she always avoided eye contact.

The bus lurched forward and Kara cursed, wishing she didn't know how the next twenty minutes would unfold: the headphones, the book, and any second now, the nodding.

Several stops later, the Walrus moved into high gear. Kara tried turning away as much as possible to avoid him, but his swaying shoulders bumped into her. The blank-faced teenager on her right, sprawled across two spaces, glanced up from thumbing his cell phone, but he refused to budge an inch.

A vigorous head-bob sent the Walrus' headphones flying onto Kara's lap; then they slipped between her legs. The Walrus opened his eyes and oriented himself. He looked between Kara's legs, lingering there for an extra second.

After months of avoidance, she found herself unable to move her eyes from his. A hint of sound from the headphones told her it wasn't The Archies.

The Walrus noticed the shift in her attention. His eyes gave a little squint and he nodded at the headphones, as if he knew her curiosity.

Kara put on the headphones.

She heard the screaming. The terror and agony behind it was so final, so complete, that the rest of the universe fell away. That a human could produce such sounds …

Her hand trembled as she ripped off the headphones. Her eyes closed for several seconds. When she opened them, she found the Walrus still sitting quietly next to her, smiling. She tried to hand the headphones to him, but the Walrus shook his head.

*No.*

She absorbed his stare, which had seemingly filled with power. Something awoke inside of her, spreading over her consciousness like molten wax.

She saw her hands put the headphones back on. Minutes later, the bus flew past Kara's stop. Her eyes were closed, and she began to nod.

# The Inconsolable Key Company

### Erik T. Johnson

Anything happened. Luke Harris tied my backpack through the fence at recess. He fished through it and tossed my pencils and notebooks around the yard. "Look, he eats his pencils, gross," he said to the gloating wall of other kids. He stood over me, laughing. They were all laughing. He shook my keys and said, "Looking for something?"

Mommy always told me never lose my keys because if something happened to me she could never forgive herself. Mommy wasn't going to be home till ten or eleven because she worked late writing wills. I asked her about wills once and she said, "You don't have to worry about that for a long time."

"Give them back," I said. "Please?"

The bell rang. Luke pocketed the keys.

"Please?" he said. He looked happy.

I couldn't concentrate during class. I had one of those brown erasers you put on top of pencils and I rolled it around in my hand and on my arms. It felt good. I shut my eyes and rubbed it on my face. When I opened my eyes it was dark outside. I sat across from two windows. I saw my reflection. I had bits of eraser all over my cheeks and forehead. I could see the buildings outside through my face. If I shifted to the side I could see one lit window behind each eye.

*That's what my ghost will look like*, I thought, *after I've rotted for a while.*

Mrs. Higgins saw. There was foam in the corner of her mouth. She asked me if I knew what I looked like.

"Yes, a dead person."

Everyone laughed.

"No," she said. "Lester Strong, you look like a fool."

The class laughed harder, Luke Harris the loudest.

"I can wash it off."

"No," she said. "You must wear it until school is over."

"Okay," I said.

After class I walked home, but knew I couldn't get in because Luke had my keys. I'd have to sit on the porch until past my bedtime. It was only three-thirty. Mommy worked late and would not be home in over seven hours.

I decided to walk a new way, crossing the widest streets I was never allowed to cross. I got to an empty dirt lot. On the other side of it was a narrow street and a street lamp blinking on and off like a giant hand was waving in front of it. It was a dead end paved with cobblestones. All the brownstones were empty and boarded up, and some were doorless and stuffed with darkness. You could hear shrill wind blowing through them like they were whistles half-full of water.

I walked to one of the brownstones. There was a beat-up black sign in a window that said THE KEY COMPANY, INC. in gold letters.

Inc. stands for Inconsolable.

I'd heard about skeleton keys that could open anything. Maybe I could find some inside and it wouldn't matter that I lost my real keys. I had to be careful that nothing happened to me, so Mommy could forgive herself. There were empty beer bottles on the stoop and crushed soda cans, and a leopard-spotted banana peel.

I peered in the doorway. I heard some kids laughing and spun around. One of them was Luke Harris. His laugh was like a hatchet cutting into Squeaky. The other two were older, pockmarked. They were tagging a deserted house across the street with spraypaint. I went through the doorway. I almost tripped on a giant metal key that I guess used to hang outside the building like a sign.

The hall was dark and musty. There was no furniture and wires stuck out of the walls.

I opened a door to the Inconsolable Key Company office. Some light dribbled from a window and onto a dead palm tree in an orange pot, and onto a black chest in the corner the size of an arcade game. There were no keys, but there was a big bowl on the middle of the floor decorated with a painting of a gold and red keyhole.

A dead man wearing clothes way too small for him came out of the painted keyhole the same way a nosebleed just appears on your shirt sometimes.

He said: "Woof. Meow. Ba-Ba."

I thought about splitting, but the kids were laughing outside. The dead man slid from the bowl. One of his legs was broke and he dragged it on the floor without sound.

"Oink," he said. "Honk."

He looked like when a fan blade spins and you can sort of see the blade but mostly it's a blur.

I wanted to run but couldn't move. He limped closer.

"Neigh. Neigh," he said. "Squeak."

His head was on backwards like a GI Joe figure thrown off a roof, but his face had slid around to the other side of his head so his eyes were looking at me. His face resembled mine with the eraser bits all over it, except his face was rotting. I think he thought I was dead because of the eraser gunk. His eye sockets were gouged out and filled with ketchup. Black holes in his eyes kept trying to force their way through.

"Choo-choo. Meow," he said, panting.

I forced myself to run behind the black chest.

The graffiti kids busted into the room with slingshots. Being afraid of monsters under the bed doesn't make sense because what about the monsters under everything else? They didn't notice me by the box. The dead man was standing in a shadow. They couldn't see him.

Luke Harris sprayed the gray plant blue. Then he went over to the box and sprayed and sprayed and then saw me and sprayed my hands while I stared at the floor.

"Hey, Six-Eyes."

It's Four-Eyes, but I didn't say anything.

Luke smacked my nose.

"Check this runt out."

I felt something squirm behind me, like muddy worms being squashed hard into my spine and the backs of my arms and neck. The dead man was rubbing himself into me. His arms were partly in my arms. His face was entering my face like how brown enters a marshmallow when you burn it.

I shouted and a slingshot rock hit my chest. It made me pull away from the dead man.

The kids were laughing and making fun of me, but I couldn't hear their words clearly, as though they were rooms away. The schoolyard was spilling through the green fences after me.

"He's sick or something. What's wrong with him?"

"The freak rubbed an eraser on his face," Luke said.

"But where's his hand, or his eye?"

They were talking about me. One of my hands was old and seethrough like a dirty window. The dead man had given me his hand. I pushed my way past the kids and I saw the dead man had one of my hands and one of my eyes. I put my Lester-hand to my right eye and it came back bloody. My eye on the dead man's face looked angry and my hand on the dead man's arm clenched into a fist.

"Moo," he said.

With my hand, he picked up the slingshot rock that hit me and threw it hard at the big kid's pimpled face. The kid fell over and crashed against the ground. He didn't move and his eyes were shut. There was a red mark like the trail of a cherry-flavored slug between his eyes.

The others got scared. I followed them but slipped in a puddle leaking from a pipe in the shadows. Luke Harris slid in it too and the kids slammed the door shut in Luke's face and I heard them jam the giant key across the door so we couldn't escape. I shook across the room as far as I could to get away from the dead man.

Luke Harris looked for a way out. I kept my real eye on the dead man. He was shambling closer and trying to tell me something. He wanted me to help him drag the kid he hit with the rock.

"Don't hurt me please," I said.

"Help me find an exit," Luke said, scratching the

glass of the barred window with my keys.

The man in shrunken clothes needed me to pull the knocked-out kid toward the bowl with the key-hole painted on it. He was pretty heavy, but I used my good hand and he used my hand and we got the kid's head to drop into the bowl. Then he pointed with my stolen hand to the top of the black box and stared at me with my eye.

I grabbed the lid with my hand and he did the same with my old hand and we lifted it. The kid on the floor moaned. The dead man put my hand in the box and pulled out a big key made of bone. It had stiff hairs growing from it in weird places. It had a sharp, beak-shaped point and hummed.

The dead man said "A, B, C, D," and walked over to the kid with his head on the bowl and shoved the bone-key into the kid's eye and turned it. The boy didn't move and the dead man chuckled with his face on backwards. I covered my real eye.

"Open," the kid with the key in his eye whispered.

I saw a door open where there wasn't a door before. The dead man in little clothes walked through. Some light filtered out of it. Luke had his back to us, but he saw the door and ran for it.

"Luke, don't do it," I said, but it was too late. He rushed through and the kid on the floor said "close" and the door shut like ventriloquist dummy lips.

I didn't want to do what I did next because I hated Luke Harris, but I thought I should try to save him so I pulled the bone-key out of the kid's eye. It shook and coughed like grandpa in the Cancer Ward. I stuck it into the kid's eye and turned it. The key sighed and the kid said "open."

The door in the wall swung open again. Mommy says there are no second chances so I figured this must be magic.

Stairs that looked like giant bad teeth descended into darkness. I lay my head on the first damp step and listened. The wind was faintly hot. Someone said "so big" in a fake baby voice and then I heard myself crying. I was there somewhere, alone and afraid. I'll bet my eye was scared of everything it saw.

"Luke," I yelled, "up here."

"Where?"

"Up here."

"Okay. You can let go of my hand, I got it."

"I don't have your hand."

He didn't answer. It was quiet for a minute and then I heard jangling. My keys flew out and landed at my feet. They were melted together into one big gloppy, inconsolable key.

I couldn't help Luke.

"Close," the kid on the floor said and he stopped breathing.

The weird door shut. I sat on the black box and took off my backpack. I pulled out a chewed pencil and a piece of loose-leaf.

I decided to write a will because Mommy told clients on the phone that having a will is important because anything can happen. At the top of the page I wrote: THE FIRST WILL AND TESTA-MENT OF LESTER STRONG. It's called a will because it's a list of stuff you're not willing to share until you're dead.

I thought about it. I didn't have anything. Then I remembered I had a hairy bone-key and a bloody gouged eye with a black hole in it.

One day someone is going to come into this room, and then they can have them.

# Eraser

## Jay MacLeod

I am in the coffee shop with Trips at three in the morning. Hayes retired for the evening several hours ago, but I am too wired to consider sleep. Trips keeps lashing my synapses with his thousand aluminum tongues and keeps drawing sweat from my pores despite the night chill. We have a long one ahead of us. Trips and I are going places. I order coffee and manage to keep down the laughter in my throat, which threatens to puncture the quiet. When the waitress gives me change, I do not look her in the eye; there's no reason to inflict us on her. I leave the shop in a cloud of stink and walk along the deserted waterfront, trying to get my bearings. This blotter is unreal.

I go several blocks before realizing where I am. I stand in front of the apartment building and look up to her windows. They are dark. The stupid bitch is probably passed out. Wake up, Ginny. Your sugar daddy's home. I fumble through my pockets for my key, but somewhere in the course of the night I have misplaced it. I enter the lobby and try to reach her on the intercom, to no avail. There is nowhere else she would be tonight. A surge of panic runs through me and I go outside. My mouth dry. Let me in, you drunk sow. Daddy needs a new pair of shoes. I take a handful of gravel and fling it against her bedroom window. After a minute, I take another handful and let it go a little harder. There is the tinkle of breaking glass. A light turns on and Ginny is in a housecoat looking like a frightened cat. I want to give her a ride and tickle her purse. Trips and I have blown our entire wad tonight and need to refuel.

"Ginny … it's Marty. Let me in."

She looks around the room stupidly and goes to the window.

"Somebody out there? Who the hell smashed my window?"

"Ginny," I say louder, "I'm sorry about the window. I had to see you. Let me in."

"Whoever you are, piss off before I call the police," she says before turning off the lights.

She's apparently blind and deaf as well.

I stand there, shivering and stupefied.

*What the fuck just happened?*

Trips isn't answering. A cop car drives past me slowly and that gets me moving. As well as being a prime candidate for the drunk / buggo tank, I have a gram in my pocket and do not need the aggravation. The cold has wrapped itself around me tightly. It was foolish to go out without a sweater. The cold inside me is much worse. Trips is giving my body the spins.

Ginny … but I try not to think about it. But she must have seen me; I was standing in the street light, clear as day.

Suddenly I am on Cogswell. I do not feel well at all. It's time I went home to try sleep. I am too wiggy to be out. All through the empty streets I hear footsteps echoing around me. I have the distinct feeling I am being observed, followed at a distance by some stranger. I look around and it's just me. Feeling like a chemical, I slink through the fog making its way from the harbor, superimposing itself over the smoke in our brain, dimming the shadows which hover in our peripheral vision.

There is no rest at the apartment. Hayes and a pack of ghouls are crowded around the coffee table playing cards and listening to Metallica as though it was the middle of the afternoon and not sun-up. Hayes looks up from his hand as if surprised to see me.

"Marty," he says, looking out of it, "I stopped at the Marquee for a couple of drinks and realized I had another hit in my wallet."

"Good, isn't it?"

He doesn't seem to hear what I am saying and continues to talk while looking past me.

"This is Eric, Joseline, Spider and Ruth. We were

about to have a smoke if you want in. Eric here has some B.C. hydro." He gestures to one of the ghouls, who are all looking up now through their long, stringy hair and eye make-up. I get the feeling that my skin has become clear and translucent. I want these mangy fuckers out of here, and Hayes to get on the next bus to New Brunswick.

*Easy does it*, I think. *These are house guests and it is the night.* I shake my head to the invitation but they have all returned their attention to the cards. I pass through the living room and into my bedroom to try and get some shuteye.

Sleep does not come easily. It never does with Trips. First there are the pains in the joints. Then the strange, creaking noises that come from inside of you. Then there are the pictures between your retinas and your eyelids activated by squidges of light which keep the darkness before sleep from being total. I toss my eyelids open and all the photographs and posters in my room leer at me. The squidges of light clutch their faces after I close my eyes again and I see them contorting, changing in shape and color.

My sheets are heavy and suffocating. I pull them off and get assailed by an arctic blast of air. My skin is grimy. Everything in my room is in an advanced stage of decay. With a strong breath I could make it all turn to dust. If I could feel my breathing. I bury my face in my pillow for what seems only a few minutes, the drug slowly releasing its grip on my body and psyche.

The sun is casting bright orange light against the white of my wall. So ends another night. I close my eyes a final time to a pair of blazing orange eyes scrutinizing my descent into unconsciousness. Sweat fills my nostrils and my breathing is mine once again.

I don't wake again until evening. Hayes is nowhere to be found and the ghouls didn't steal anything. The night is off to a fine start. I discover on the answering machine that I missed a job interview, which doesn't mean dick as it was only for a job at a fast food joint. Times are getting lean, however. In the mailbox is a cutoff warning from the power company to match the one I got a few days ago for the telephone. I have to do something.

I call Ginny on my way to her apartment. We have a glass of wine; I have one and she has four, while she goes on about some freak who broke her window last night. Having these chats before sex makes her feel a little better about our relationship. Normally, I humor her and feign interest in whatever she's talking about. More often than not she's lamenting her husband who turned queer and left her, and her son who never calls her anymore. The son is quite a bit like me, actually.

"So you didn't get a look at him, then?"

"For just a minute I thought it might have been you; his voice sounded like yours, but …"

She gets a far-off look in her eyes as if she's remembering the life she used to have as a devoted, non-alcoholic mother and wife living in an upper-middle class neighborhood with last year's model in the two-car garage. That was ten years ago.

"He was about your height and build, but he didn't look anything like you."

"But he said my name."

Why is it so difficult to get a straight answer? Why don't I tell her it was me?

"It couldn't have been you," she says with certainty, putting her hand on my leg. A smile creeps across her face. "And now that you mention it, I don't think he said your name. I was quite under the spell last night."

"Under the spell." That's a riot. "I don't remember much."

"Incidentally," she says, unbuttoning my fly, "your friend came by earlier this afternoon. Hayes. He told me he was afraid he kept you last night. He's a nice young man."

So now she ups the stakes by implicating Hayes. This bitch is going mental. It may soon be time for Marty to move on. It was definitely a mistake for me to introduce them. I thought it might be a wise way to palm her off. That was at the other end of a two week bender. I need her for her money again and she knows it.

*These head games will not avail her*, I think as she slides off my jeans and throws them to the floor. The booze made her buggy last night and now she's out to get me. What the hell is going on? I think about her wallet as I do my part and unbutton her blouse. Then I am on top of her on the couch.

After a few minutes, I have to stop. Ginny isn't pleased. She tries to heat me up but nothing is happening; I am hopelessly flaccid. Eventually she stops trying and goes to the bathroom. I take this opportunity to rummage through her purse. There is nothing in her wallet except for a couple of fives. Damn it and damn it again. Yesterday was alimony day. Something is off kilter.

"Say, darling," I say when she gets out, trying to sound casual, "you don't have a few dollars to lend me so I can buy some food and pay a couple bills?"

"Are you still here?" She seems genuinely surprised. "No, I'm pretty tapped."

"I was out all day job hunting and was hoping to go out with the boys for a beer or two."

Normally this is good for thirty or forty dollars.

"Sorry dear," she says and kisses me coyly. "I should be getting some rest. Some of us have to get up in the morning, you know."

*What the fuck.*

"I'd sure like to stay with you tonight, Ginny."

Normally this would go against every instinct I possess.

"Sorry, Marty, but a He-Man like you would keep me up all night." She passes me my clothes and disappears into her bedroom. "Lock the door on the way out, won't you?"

*Ginny*, I think desperately, *don't do this to me.*

Something vital has happened to her agenda. Something to make her think she is in control. She

will come back to me and I will show her no re-
morse.

I leave her apartment in a hurry, but not before I
take money from her purse. I walk, intending to get
a beer somewhere, anywhere that I might get lost.
I'll have to sort out Hayes the next time I see him.

Inside I am a tightly wound coil of anxiety
and once more I have the sensation of being followed. The footsteps I hear—a half-pace behind
mine—rise above the noise of pedestrians, cars and
thoughts. My limbs feel utterly weightless. This is
not Trips, but what else could it be? My vision blurs
and I am about to fall.

Darkness rushes to catch me.


I dream that I am being erased. I am a flat stick
figure on a piece of paper drawn inside of a box.
A hand emerges from the void above and extends
the boundaries of the box with a pencil. Inside the
newly extended boundary of the box, another stick
figure is drawn. The pencil is upturned and goes
to work erasing me. I am stuck between pencil and
paper. I can't even scream as my constituent parts
disappear, one stick at a time.

*Eyes see:*

> *Marty,*
>> *thin and weak,*
>>> *walking down the*

*sidewalk.*
*He falls down.*

*He gets up, keeps walking.*

*Feet:*

> *walk,*

>> *follow Marty.*

*: continue to replace Marty*

I wake in my room. The sun is shining and I feel dull and groggy, alarmed in my stupor. I have no idea how I got here. My room is different. Several of my posters are missing. I pull myself out of bed and force myself into the living room. My stereo has disappeared, along with my coffee table.

*What the fuck?*

The door rattles and Hayes walks up the stairs. He pushes past me as though I am not even there.

"Hayes …"

My voice is weak and raspy. I have to fight for every word.

"I came by to grab my things," he says crisply. "I'm catching the next bus home." He begins to stuff his clothes into a duffel bag. "That was some tangent you were on last night."

"I don't remember."

"I'm not surprised, the shape you were in. You said ridiculous things. You've turned into a drag, Marty."

"My things …"

I point to where my stereo used to be.

"I haven't a clue. You don't sound too well." He

looks at me, past me, squinting as though trying to make something out. "You don't look too well." He zips his bag, tosses it over his shoulder and roots through his pockets. "Maybe you should lay off the shit for awhile."

"I seem to have misplaced the house key. Sorry." He grins and jogs down the stairs. "You should treat Ginny better. She's a wonderful lady."

My sore head is full of questions.

I go into the bathroom and what I see in the mirror makes me ill. It isn't me, but someone of the same height and build. His skin—this thing— is yellow and jaundiced. I move my hand and the thing moves its hand, the gesture delayed by a fraction of a second.

Perhaps I am still tripping. The thought is almost comforting.

I leave the bathroom. My living room is now completely barren. Through a broken window I see the very edge of the setting sun. I try to turn on the light as the apartment fills with darkness, but the power's been shut off. I try to cry out, but I have no voice left with which to scream. The room shrinks until it is only a pin prick, a squidge of light in the dark.

It is the shadow of a hand. My hand.

I am erased.

# Sweaters

## Dan Florkowski

I loathed every shopper that swarmed my store:
the young and the old, the Dutch and the Apache,
women in pointy red shoes and men in penny loaf-
ers. Their appearance played no effect on my judg-
ment. I despised them equally.

Every day they'd come in and never buy a thing.
They'd skillfully fuck up my neat stacks of clothes
as if they had trained for it, leaving behind sweater sandwiches for me to clean. A tuna burger was
a pink sweater mashed between two brown; the
Big Mac was a dark brown, red, green and yellow
between two tan; the works was all twelve colors
crushed in no particular order. Only a true deli
master could construct the latter. I was fortunate
enough to run across one every week or so.

Before lunch, I'd break apart these thoughtful
gifts and reorganize the ingredients into their re-

DAN PIORKOWSKI

spective stacks. But when I'd come back, the sweaters would be intermingled like the colors of a rainbow crayoned by a three-year-old with cataracts.

"It's useless," I'd tell my partner. Unlike me, he was able to work up enough courage to leave the business—a courage that came a few months after his wife and bratty children left him. He was a good father and worked hard to put food on the table. But his slut of a wife didn't give a damn about integrity and left him for someone richer. The kids would tell him they loved their new daddy's house more because it had a pool. "What a bullshit excuse," I told him. We lived in Minnesota and the water was glazed over in ice for the majority of the year.

I came in early one morning and all the stacks of cashmere sweaters were perfectly folded. The colors were coordinated appropriately and the floor was swept clean of all food court trash. I closed the previous night and left everything a mess because my bottle of scotch was more enticing than folding a perpetual pile of clothing, but that morning the store looked like it had fallen out of a catalog. It was in a perfect state—clean and free of customers.

Porn was playing on the computer in the back office. That's where I found my partner hanging from the ceiling fan with a belt around his neck and a chair tipped over on the floor. His pants were missing and his dick was still hard. The video on the screen was five minutes in.

I deleted the porn from the computer and

62

reported it as a suicide. I didn't want his slut of an ex-wife telling everyone that her ex-husband had killed himself masturbating. A few weeks later, a letter from City Hall arrived stating that my partner left me his half of the store and the privilege of folding twice as many sweaters. I would have followed in the wake of his footsteps, but I didn't have the balls to kill myself without someone cheering me on.

My alarm clock rang every morning and its beeping marked the beginning of my daily prison sentence. I served every minute with honor until I lost consciousness in my bed at night. I never dreamed, not even as a child. And soon after my partner died, I considered myself happiest when my mind was inactive. Each new day brought a more appealing viewpoint on death. A never-ending nap of nothingness. No people, no mall, no sweaters. Death contained the freedom I sought.

I told one of the schmucks fucking up my store that he could have all the sweaters if he killed me. He thought it was a joke. He came back the next day to make more sandwiches because he had nothing better to do. I asked him sixty-three separate times before he agreed.

Around midnight we went to the city dump. We walked past mounds of broken glass, old baby strollers and shredded tires. I circled and inspected the mounds of garbage until I found the spot. It was a half-filled ditch of Styrofoam hidden behind a stack of smashed plasma televisions.

I pointed to the Styrofoam and said, "This is where I want to die."

I tossed him the keys to the shop and a pistol I bought from a pawn shop. He clicked off the safety, raised the gun and blessed himself. Then he pulled the trigger and a bullet burrowed between my eyebrows. It was glorious.

I enjoyed the blackness of death. I liked the cold. The frigid atmosphere soothed the wounds that seeped deep into my soul while I was still trapped in my mortal body. Months—if not years—later, I opened my eyes and wandered around. I wasn't alone. There were other lost souls stuck in this purgatory; I just didn't know it yet. I wished I had never opened my eyes. It would have been better than knowing the truth.

My abdomen emitted a light that illuminated twenty paces worth of the nothingness ahead of me. I walked for days on a substance that felt like dirt but didn't stick to the soles of my feet. The image my eyes processed never changed. It was always twenty paces and then darkness, a canvas dunked in crude oil. There was nothing lively about it. I was naïve to consider it my own utopia.

Eventually I found a sidewalk and both directions seemed to go on forever. But forever just meant longer than twenty paces. I picked a direction and walked. The path was smooth and there weren't any breaks in the concrete. It was more similar to a uniform slab of marble than anything else. I never considered venturing onto the soil. The path presented a purpose, as if there was something at the end waiting for me.

Sometime later, a faint light from another body approached from the distance. Forty paces from each other, our lights merged. The other's light was duller than mine. He stopped a few feet away from me.

His eyes were two ebony orbs the size of golf balls buried under a thin layer of whiteness that composed his entire body. He said something, but nothing on his face moved. I paused for a moment to collect myself and then realized neither of us had orifices. We no longer had a need to breathe, eat, or reproduce. He bowed his hole-less head at me and I did the same. Then he extended his mitt-like hand. He had an opposable thumb, but the other four digits were fused together. My hands were the same. We shook flippers and he welcomed me to the new world.

We walked the opposite direction I was going. He said I was traveling the wrong way and after several days of silence I asked where we were going.

"The store."

"The store? But we're ghosts."

"There's a lot of stuff ghosts need."

"Like what?"

"Things to pass time, like jigsaw puzzles and model airplanes."

"You're kidding."

"Look around you. This darkness is all you'll see for the rest of time. And don't bother thinking about the good days on Earth, 'cause that won't help. You'll never be able to go back."

"That's fine. I don't want to go back."

"Go walk in the shadows for a while. You'll change your mind. We all do."

He patted my back with his flipper and we journeyed further into the eternal darkness.

"You couldn't pay me to go back to the mall," I said.

"The mall?" He stopped walking. "Why didn't you tell me you've been to the end of the path?" He took a step closer and lifted something off his torso and his light grew as bright as mine. "Did you happen to see the sweaters? They're fantastic."

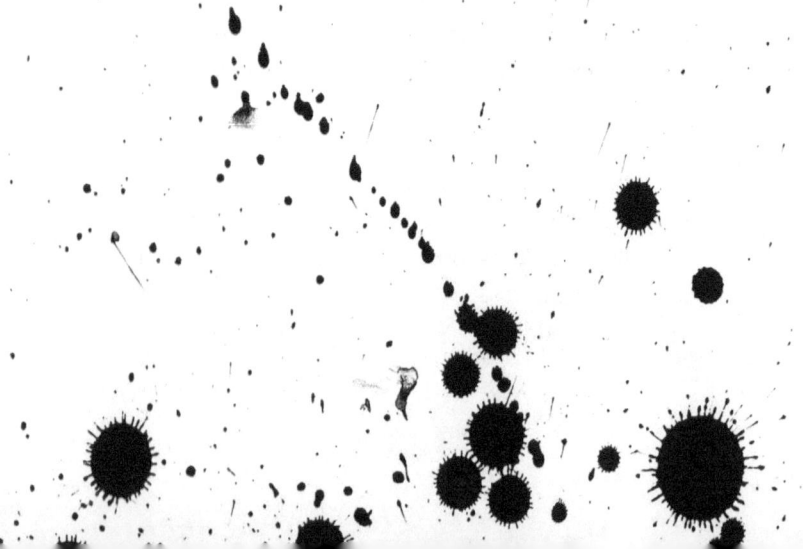

# Moonman

## Kristine Ong Muslim

It wasn't our fault. You should understand that by now. But I don't expect you to understand the reason we did what we thought we had to do that summer because people don't understand order as much as we do.

At first, there were three of us: Mel Arlington, Judith Legold, and me. By the end of the semester before that summer vacation, Billy Gambale, a fourth-grader who once helped Mel push my bicycle out of the ditch, joined our little group. I could never forget that day. It was humid, and the whole world was the mighty Godzilla out to get us. The burly Bartman and his ferocious pack were chasing me and Mel—riding double with me on my bike. I lost control of the handlebars when we reached the embankment so we landed in the ditch near Mr. Ashley's farm. The Bartman and his gang were laughing their heads off as they walked away from us. Mel and I cursed silently as we eased our way out of the filthy mud bath.

We both understood that we had no choice but to endure the treatment, because that was how the world worked. There was so much room for pain because the course of natural hierarchy—the taut demarcation line that separated predator from prey—had to be sustained that way. We knew that. We respected that.

"Want some help?" the freckled Billy Gambale called out from the embankment.

According to Judith, Billy spent almost half of his life playing inside the video arcade at Kingshoppe because he didn't have any friends. He flushed, probably thinking that it would be a lot easier if we ignored him.

"Come down if you want to," Mel said, laughing and splashing mud on me. "You're Billy, right?"

"Yeah."

He brightened instantly. I could swear I'd never seen happiness as profuse as that which shone from Billy Gambale's eyes.

That afternoon at Judith's house, Billy watched *Flame of Recca*—a Japanese animated series—with us. We ate chocolate cookies and drank all the milk in the fridge.

There were four of us in the Legolds' spacious living room and the thought of us being friends for a lifetime suddenly sank into me.

It was on the twenty-fifth of June when we first

ventured into the vacant lot beside the Lares House to play baseball. It was Billy's turn to pitch.

Judith swung for the fences.

*Crack.*

I followed the ball's course across the sky even though the sun hurt my eyes. Strange, but I felt like a real man whenever I did that. It landed somewhere in the middle of the thick vegetation fifteen feet away from us.

Mel went for the ball. He told us earlier that he managed to snatch it from his older brother's bedroom because his brother had his head clamped with headphones. "The volume was so high you could hear the sound from the next room," Mel said. "I think he'll need a hearing aid the size of a boom box when he gets older."

We all laughed at that.

Mel was approaching the bushes when Judith screamed. I never heard her scream before; she was as hard-assed as any man I'd ever seen in my life.

Mel froze. Following the direction of Billy's frightened gaze, I saw it: a white face with holes lurking sparsely on its surface. It looked like a child, but its face resembled something out of a whiteboard cutout, with eyes made of buttons, a paper clip nose, and a piece of string shaped to form the lips. Most of all, there were those terrible, hateful spots on his skin which resembled miniature lunar craters.

Mel stepped backward as the creature took one step forward. Its grotesque limbs were holding the ball, stretching them awkwardly Mel's direction to indicate that it wanted to return the ball.

My three friends huddled closer to me, their eyes fixed on the creature as it set the ball on the third base and left. Judith was the one who picked it up for Mel.

"I think he's just a freak," Mel said, looking down at his dirty sneakers as we walked away from the Lares House.

"He must've gotten radiation when he was a kid," Billy added.

I was annoyed by the way that they blatantly referred to the creature as a *he*. It wasn't human to me. And I hated it, had to hate it more for what it represented. It was completely dislodged from my concept of primal order. The creature was an abomination, like a punk clad in a motorcycle jacket and engineer boots mouthing nothing but the f-word. And when you were a kid, it was not easy to allow it to fit into your general scheme of things or accept even the remotest possibility of its existence. It was too much for me.

"What's radiation?" Judith asked.

"It causes things to mutate," Billy said. "Like if I give it to you, you'll change into a rat or something."

"Shit," Mel said, horrified. "How do you get it?"

"I don't know," Billy answered. "It's everywhere. The government puts it on our food so we don't get past fifty. And there's this one time—"

"I think it's an alien invader," I told them. I was

not smiling. I knew they realized I meant business. "I think it wants to take over the world. We have to stop it."

"Us?" Mel gasped. His face was ashen with fear.

"Don't you think we have to call 911?" Judith said.

"I guess you're right, Jude," Billy agreed.

"They won't believe us. Not grown-ups. They won't believe a thing like that. They'd laugh their heads off and then stick us in the loony bin like Carl's dad."

"Not if we take a picture of him," Judith suggested.

I noticed that Mel was nervous.

"How?" I said. "Say 'hey, Mr. Moonman, we'd like you to pose and say cheese because we need to take a nice picture of you and send it to *X-Files*.'"

"Why don't we just forget about him, okay?" Mel said. He was sweating.

We were silent after that.

"Come here tomorrow," I said when we reached my house. All I wanted was to become a leader, a real man. I would take the responsibility if I had to. We'd talk about what we're supposed to do.

I walked across the yard. I didn't wait for them to say something because I knew they would stick with me no matter what happened.

In the end, everyone agreed to join me in hunting the thing and killing it. Mel, anxious about the idea, finally gave in when he saw Judith's enthusiastic response.

We tracked down the Moonman for three days without success. On the fourth day, we had the luck to spot it near the stream, forming a mound of sand with its bulbous fingers. That scene disturbed me; no other kind of blasphemy could come closer to it. The creature was building what appeared to be a sandcastle.

It did not have a right to do that as much as it was devoid of its right to exist. The Moonman had corrupted my innocence, and I thought I had nothing else to lose after that. I pegged my first rock with such murderous force that my arm ached in its socket that night. The rock hit the creature squarely on the forehead and it collapsed against the stream bank.

*Yes, close your eyes now, Moonman*, my mind was shouting triumphantly. *Close your eyes and seal those lunar craters on your skin forever. Let the earth feed on you and leave us in peace.*

Then I saw red stuff oozing out of its hairless head. I could not believe what I saw but I knew it was blood.

Mel cried.

All three of his rocks fell out of his shirt.

*Thud, thud, thud*: colder than the earth, they whispered a rhythmic chant as they hit the ground.

"It was only a freak," Judith said to herself. "We're murderers."

Billy and Mel quickly found their way out of the dense undergrowth we used as a hiding place. They ran. Away. They never talked to me after that.

Judith cried on our way home, and I never heard a word from her again. But I knew they had kept the secret. It was a pact none of us needed to talk about.

A month after the incident, I overheard my father talking to my mother about a decayed body near the stream two miles from the Lares House. According to my father, the police swore they never thought the remains could be that of a human's until it was autopsied.

But I knew better.

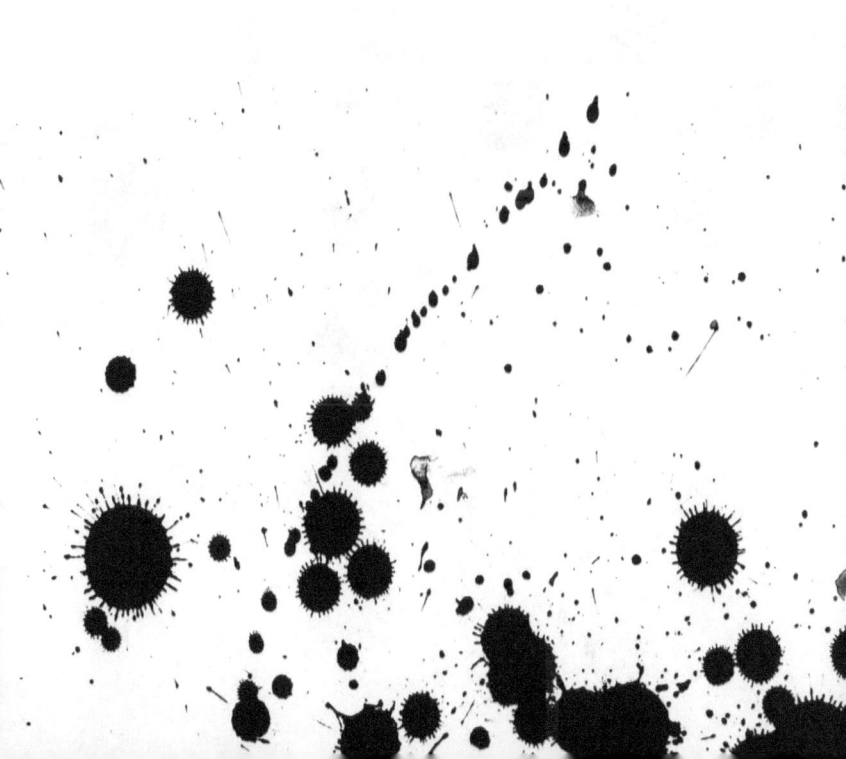

# Behind The Walls

## Amanda Larson

Elle slid the knife blade experimentally over his finger. He hissed at the initial burning sensation, but then pressed at the slit skin, watching with a detached curiosity as the crimson swelled to the surface and seeped from the wound. It would seem a shame that he planned on wasting so many liters of blood, but no one wanted his filthy plasma. He should have put a biohazard sign at the door.

It was a little late for that now. The knife from the pawnshop was as sharp as the salesman had promised. He assured it would slide through a deer's gut. It was an odd selling point. Elle had never even seen a deer. He imagined not many in the middle of the city hunted animals.

His eyes roamed the etched graffiti and dubious smudges on the surface of the glass. He made a note of the missing wall tiles and chipped paint on the bathroom stalls behind him. Every part of the reflection was scrutinized except for the one thing he was avoiding—himself.

Reluctantly, a set of bloodshot eyes met the ones staring back at him. Cheap mascara left dark smudges under sunken eyes hiding behind purple shadow. Cheekbones formed gaunt, sickly wells leading to lips accentuated in liner. A fading bruise decorated one of the cheeks, though the tousled, half shoulder-length hair and a hefty helping of cover-up disguised it well enough.

A lot of things went through Elle's mind as he trailed the reflection to the scrawny, nearly naked body attached to it. The question that screamed the loudest in his mind was whether or not slitting his wrists would be faster than slitting his throat.

He had almost asked the man in the pawnshop for his opinion. There was little doubt in his mind that he would have sold him the knife anyway.

The girl named Elaine had been his mother's myth. It was easy when he was younger, back when a bob-cut and a Hello Kitty skirt could fool the masses.

Then came puberty. By that point, even his own mother—who had hated men with a passion, enough so to deny that her own son would one day become one—could no longer stand the sight of him. She had given up the lie, though by then it was the only truth he had known.

The world had no place for Elaine Elliot.

Even before he had become sick and quit his

sordid occupation, they had stopped paying for what he offered. Everyone wanted the kid, not some used-up young man. If he had gone to school or learned a legitimate trade, maybe he could have moved on, but after his mother overdosed, Elle had managed to hide from the grasps of foster care. He never so much as stayed in a house overnight and, for better or worse, raised himself. Now he was unable to do even that.

Either way, he was dying. It was a matter of time. AIDS was a slow, ugly death. He had watched friends waste away. If he could somehow get access to medication, he might still be able to live a long life, but no one was going to treat him and he was too tired to start over.

His choice was between a lingering death on the streets and the relatively quick death of draining his own blood. While bleeding to death would take a while, it would not take years. A well-placed bullet would be faster, but a knife was a hell of a lot easier to obtain than a gun.

Elle was unsure if he'd be able to make a second cut after the first. If he damaged the tendons, his hand might not work well enough to grip the knife. He could try propping the handle between his knees and drag his other wrist across, but if he screwed up, would one cut be enough?

Wandering thoughts silenced at the grinding of rusted hinges. Reflexively, his fingers tightened on the hilt of the knife. The dingy public bathroom was usually deserted at these hours, and locked.

The guilt of knowing some poor sap would have to clean the mess of his dead body in the morning compounded when a young woman entered the bathroom. She was far too gorgeous to be walking through the night alone. A few minutes later and she would have stumbled on him bleeding out on the floor—a horrid night for them both.

"Oh, sorry," Elle muttered. "Do you need ... I can go."

He forgot he was standing in his briefs gripping a nasty knife. While his bony form was not exactly intimidating, he had to appear insane. Technically he was, yet the woman appeared unfazed.

With the grace of an angel, she approached. Her hair cascaded in lush wavy locks past her shoulders. Her curves and the gentle sway of her hips were perfection. The way the slim, low-cut black dress clung to her was something to be envied.

Elle could tell by the way she held herself that she was not working the streets. He knew that life inside-out; no one living it possessed the kind of self-assurance she emanated.

When she spoke, her tone was silk.

"You know what they say: 'go down the high-way, not across the road.'" She leaned against the sink, hands casually at her hips. "If you go across, you'll destroy the tendons. The throat would be faster, but it's an unsightly way to go."

It took him a moment to process the words. She couldn't be real. The stunning woman did not so much as cast a reflection in the mirror.

"You wanted to overdose. Why the knife?"

She was right. He had tried to overdose, but he couldn't even do *that* right. And a knife had sounded harder to screw up.

When he did not answer aloud, she continued regardless. "Wrist-slitting has a low rate of success." She could have been discussing weather. "Usually it's a cry for help."

"Who are you?"

"Help," she replied. "Or at least I *can* be if you let me."

Despite his mind shutting down, or possibly because of it, he set the knife onto the crusted sink ledge.

A ghost smile graced her lips. She shook her head, motioned for the knife.

"Don't leave it here. A young pregnant girl was beaten tonight. Natisha. She lost the baby. Tomorrow morning she'll come in here and find your body and the knife."

"How could you know that?"

"She's one of mine. Like you. She will find another way to me, but your conscience is heavy enough already."

Her eyes bore to the center of his soul, as if she could see everything he had spent his life trying to hide.

"Even *you* didn't know," she told him, "until they found you in the dumpster and ran those tests at the hospital. You didn't know you were sick."

His heart dropped as he brought an unsteady

hand to his mouth. He uselessly wiped the corner of his eyes that again tickled with tears he refused to release.

There was no way she could know that.

She could have easily made up the story about the little girl, but how could she possibly know the weight he'd carried of the countless men he had potentially infected before knowing he was a carrier? They were scumbags, but many had families. Those families would be destroyed because of him.

Elle vehemently shook his head, unable to form the words to deny it.

She pulled his trembling body against hers. He tried to twist away, but his limbs were weak, and while she did not force her hold physically, something about her tenderness made it impossible to rebuke it.

"You can't hurt me," she said, as if reading his mind. "If you come with me, I can protect you."

She stepped back far enough to extend a hand. He had nothing to lose by taking it. No matter how much she wanted to help, she could not help him outrun himself.

Her skin was cold, but the warmth of her smile balanced it out. He honestly did not care what her disorienting touch offered as long as it was a way out.

Her touch brought flashes of light that he could almost discern as images. Most were blurry and distorted, but for a brief moment he thought he saw his collapsed body on the floor.

When he could again focus, Elle found himself flat against a tiled floor with a feeling that he had been pulled a great distance. He was still in a bathroom, though. The cool floor against his cheek was immaculately clean. It smelled foreign with a hint of lemon, rather than the rancid odor of booze and piss. It might still be a bathroom, but it was not the same one.

The bathroom was opulent, at least by his standards. It was big enough to live out of, the lights bright, the walls pristine with no traces of graffiti, and the bathtub could serve as a small swimming pool. A basket of soaps and a plush robe waited by a stack of fluffy white towels. He had seen a bathroom like this once before at an old, upscale hotel. As ridiculous as it would seem to most, he had loved that bathroom.

Bewilderment flooded over him as he realized this was the exact bathroom. His mind was playing tricks on him. That old hotel was demolished years ago.

Disoriented, Elle stumbled to his feet.

The knife remained on the floor. The skin on the finger he had cut minutes earlier was immaculate. The chipped polish on his nails was now a smooth coat. His fingers perfectly manicured.

He stood frozen at the mirror. Bright eyes, beautifully rounded cheeks, full lips and healthy bronzed skin. The hair was not the stringy, hand-combed mess he had expected, but shiny and full. He reached out disbelievingly. The person staring back did the same.

It took time to get over the reflection, but when he did, he walked out of the bathroom in hopes of finding something that made sense. Impossible as it seemed, he was in the hotel he so fondly remembered from long ago.

He saw the same astonishing city lights from the first time he stood at the window. He had dreamed of watching the sunrise from such a height.

There was a large vanity in the room, a mahogany desk, wing-back chairs and a flat screen television. He couldn't remember the old hotel having one. The familiar, oversized bed was perfectly made with clean bedding.

A dress has been pristinely laid out over the covers. The same black dress worn by the woman in the bathroom.

Elle held it to the vanity, where he discovered his cheeks were not the only thing that had filled out. Unable to resist, he slid on the dress. The light fabric draped elegantly over his new hips and revealed ample breasts. The woman in the mirror was beautiful.

"It really is you," said a voice.

Elle spun on his heels. The woman from the bathroom stood behind him, her hands folded. She smiled.

Elle could not stop his features from twisting in confusion.

"What did you do?" he asked.

"I let you see what you want to see. Welcome

home, Elaine."

He was not all that interested in making sense of it. He was too afraid that understanding would bring it to an end. Instead, he returned to the mirror and the woman behind him was gone.

Sometime later, Elle gathered the courage to leave the room and headed into the empty hallway. It was not long before a voice called out from behind him.

"Hey, gorgeous, wait up!"

Years of conditioning told him no one would call him gorgeous with a straight face, but he was the only one in the hallway.

An older woman hustled over. She had a shaved head and was solidly built. Her tank top showed off defined biceps and the ornate tribal tattoos decorating her arms. Work boots clunked heavily against the hardwood floor

"You must be the new girl," she said.

"I guess I am. It's Elle … Elaine."

"Karen. It's awesome to meet you.." The woman set a hand on his shoulder. A comforting smile filled her face. "There's a hell of a party downstairs. You up for a good time?"

"What's the occasion?"

"Every night's a party. You've hit the clubs, right?"

Elle nodded.

A few clubs downtown didn't check IDs, which was a must because he didn't have one. Nor did he have the cash to splurge on a forgery. Clubs were open late and they let him put off the dark alleys a few hours longer. In the dim light and blind hustle of bodies, he could blend in … just exist.

"Think of your favorite club and this is a hundred times better. Come on, this is going to blow your mind."

They waited for an elevator at the end of the hallway. The lift was modern and completely out of place, considering the old hotel elevators had the manual accordion style doors. There was nothing in the hallway that resembled the old hotel except for the beige wallpaper. When the elevator door slid open, a bellhop waited inside. The man's presence made Karen laugh.

Several floors lower, the elevator opened to a grand lobby. He recognized the chandeliers, but not much else. They passed a large room with buffet tables where old men in suits were schmoozing with each other over glasses of wine—men he was hoping not to find here.

"That's not our party, Elaine."

Karen pulled open one of the double-doors. He slipped inside, instantly embracing the riotous, musical bass thumping through the floorboards. The room flashed brilliantly with colored stage lights. A familiar, smoky haze filled the air.

Some inside looked like standard club regulars; others were starkly out of place.

"That's David," Karen said loudly into Elle's ear.

She pointed to a man in a designer suit trying to dance with a sassy underdressed woman half his age. He could not move in rhythm with the music to save his life. His tie was loose and the sleeves of his dress shirt were rolled. A jacket draped over an arm.

"He may look like one of the stiffs, but the boy knows how to have a good time."

The party was everything he had expected of a night out at the club. All of the good and none of the bad.

Hardly any time passed before the sun's glow tinted the sky outside. He hadn't noticed the window until late in the evening, but he was glad it was there. Perched at the bar, he watched the sun rise above the city. It was even more magnificent than he had imagined.

"I don't want to leave," he told Karen.

"Oh sweetie." She pulled him into a hug. "Didn't she tell you? You're already home."

Elle pulled back in surprise. She held up her hand to stop him before he could speak.

"Don't ask me where or how. I don't know. I don't even care. That lady pulled me out of hell and I'm not about to look a gift horse in the mouth."

While Elle had let Karen go at that, he could not leave it alone and spent the next several hours exploring the hotel. He met a lot of people. Some scared him, some refused to leave their rooms and some kept disappearing. Most were nice, quirky people. They were all odd and he enjoyed that, but still he did not understand.

They all spoke in past tense.

When he found Karen again, she was lining a shot on a pool table in a game room. There was no indirect way to present the question on his mind.

"Are we all suicides?"

Karen stopped just short of tapping the cue ball. She was slightly taken aback, but not startled at the question.

The theory so clear in his mind was brought into question by a little girl playing tea party underneath the pool table. She appeared no older than six and was involved in a whispered conversation with an antique doll.

"She can't be," he said, mostly to himself.

The little girl's eyes were disturbingly old.

"I was sixty seven when I drowned in the bathtub."

Elle struggled with a reply to help close his gapping mouth.

"Oh. Well … you look good for your age."

She giggled and set her doll aside. After scampering out from beneath the table, she straightened the wrinkles from her old-fashioned lacy dress. A sweet smile spread across her face as she patted Elle's hand.

"You're a sweet boy," she said. "This is what I wanted."

"To be a little kid?"

"To be cute again."

Elle didn't have time to consider her reply before Karen groaned, "Oh, come on!"

A vase of cut sunflowers rested on the center of

the pool table. That was not as odd as the fact that the pool table had transformed into a hardwood dining room table. One by one, the pool balls rolled off with heavy clunks to the floor.

Karen tapped her foot impatiently.

The not-so-young girl squealed with joy and hurried to the door where a teenage girl had entered. The new girl was maybe sixteen. Her skin was intensely dark and her black hair was tucked neatly behind her ears. She had a pierced brow and wore a long skirt that her swollen belly hung out over. As she stood in the doorway, her hand rubbed protectively over her exposed stomach.

"Natisha!" the little girl announced, wrapping her arms around the woman's legs.

"Hey, Stephanie."

Her voice was soft, maybe even a little shy, but it was her name that brought the uneasy feeling to the pit of Elle's stomach.

Hurried footsteps echoed from the hallway, followed by an urgent shout. "There's a meeting in Room 412 convening in five minutes! Don't be late!" A moment later the message repeated as the man ran further down the hall.

Karen rolled her eyes.

"That's Bryan." She said it as though the simple statement alone was all the explanation needed. "He's going to save us."

"From what?"

"You'll see. I wish someone would save us from him. As much as I'd love to ignore his crazy ass, when no one shows at his meetings, he keeps moving the time back until someone does. Let's go, it'll be good for a laugh."

When they reached Room 412, David—the horrid dancer from the nightclub—was grudgingly dragged into the room by a man Elle assumed was Bryan. The man had a prematurely receding hairline. The hair he had was wild and he had a scraggly beard to match. He wore oversized sweatpants and a sleeveless shirt probably white once upon a time.

There were no furnishings in the room, except for the scarred wood chair sitting ominously in the corner. The carpet was discolored with stains, but it was the bricked-over window that made the hair on the nape of Elle's neck stand on end. A flickering bare bulb cast long, disorienting shadows.

Bryan shoved the door closed. His fingers trying to fasten a long line of security chains. Bryan checked the deadbolt before grabbing the rickety chair from the corner and propping it beneath the doorknob.

"What are you doing?" David asked.

The well-dressed man sounded bored, absently swirling some amber colored liquid in a crystal glass.

"Keeping *her* out," Bryan said. "The one who trapped us here."

"The woman that saved our lives?" Elle asked.

"Woman … saved us … *oh boy*." Bryan's clipped words were followed by a humorless chuckle. His bony, nicotine-stained fingers wrung through his hair. The jittery man was either on something heavy or long overdue for a hit. "She's got you all under her spell. I'm telling you, she does."

Bryan paced over an established, worn pattern on the carpet.

"None of us can leave," he said.

The strangled frustration in his voice further unnerved Elle.

"Am I the only one that gets this?"

"Hey, man, calm down," Elle said.

"Try seeing yourself comatose, and then *you* calm the fuck down!"

Karen stepped forward. "Seriously, listen to the sister. If you don't take meditation or find yourself a boatload of Valium, there's going to be a stroke in your future."

"You think I'm lying?"

"No, we think you're *crazy*," David replied. He took a sip from the glass in his hand as he leaned against the wall.

"He's not wrong," Natisha said quietly. She was standing at the back of the room with her arm wrapped around the little girl. "I saw it too. I saw *me*."

"Great. There has to be a gas leak in here," Karen said. She gave a distasteful look to the rotted, paint-peeling walls. "Or toxic mold."

David scowled and pushed away from the wall. He brushed off his suit while Karen unblocked the door.

"Why don't you step outside then?" Bryan

moved behind Karen, practically yelling in her ear. "Go for a walk and get some fresh air. Oh wait, you *can't*."

Before Karen could take a swing, Elle asked, "Why would we want to leave?"

"A person should be able to go wherever they want," Bryan said. "I tried jumping out a window, and do you know what happened?"

"A parachute shot out of your ass?"

Karen set the chair aside and unlatched the door locks.

"No. I woke up in my bed!"

"Oh my god," she gasped mockingly. "Me too, you moron. It's called dreaming."

All of this was like a dream.

The argument continued, but Elle had stopped listening. The others were gone. Everything was gone. He was in his room. The bed beneath him shifted slightly as someone sat beside him.

"Bryan has lost a large part of himself."

It was the woman who brought him here. He never had to speak aloud for her to know what was on his mind.

"Why does he think he's in a coma?"

She set her hand over his.

"Because he is."

"Am *I?*"

She shook her head.

Elle pursed his lips and said, "The little girl thinks she's dead."

"Do you *feel* dead?"

"Not anymore. But this place isn't real."

"You're protected here." She smiled softly. "You aren't dead, and these rooms … they are *not* places. Come here. If you want to know, you can see."

She ushered him to the mirror and he saw his reflection there once again. It was still unfamiliar, yet in a way more familiar and true than his normal reflection.

Soon it was less like he was looking at a mirror and more like he was looking through a window.

"Who's that?" Elle asked.

Through the glass was a man getting ready for work.

"That's Elliot, the part of you that you rejected. Who you are here is who you wanted to be, who you couldn't be out there."

"Then where am I?"

"The same place you have always been." She tapped her finger against his temple to illustrate her point. "What you chose was not to come *with* me, but to let me in. *I'm* the guest here."

"Everyone here, they're all in my head?"

"No. They are as real as you. This room is yours. The rest of this place—the shared areas—are a culmination of what all of you imagine. When you invited me in, I did a little remodeling. I built a wall between your warring aspects and added some new passageways so none of you would be alone."

The grimace deepened on the reflected man's face.

"He's still dying. I'm still dying. The people I—"

She squeezed his hand to silence him.

"All fruits start rotting the moment they are picked. You can't change that. No one can, but here you can live, and out there so can *he* … for the time you are both allowed. You were right. You can't run from yourself, but I can hide you."

# Creature

Aaron J. French

Harry's mother had an accident while crossing the street. Now she lay in a hospital bed clinging to life. This was the end. Once she died, the creature would get free. That meant more children were going to die.

He hated thinking about it. Machines were keeping her alive. She was never going to wake. Even if she did, the machines had caused severe brain damage. It was a matter of "when" and Harry was supposed to decide this "when."

Here came Doctor Reynolds now. Short brown hair, glasses, skin smooth as butter.

*How easily it comes apart—long ribbons of meat—blood—flesh—*

Hansel's thinking. The creature.

"How you holding up, Harry?" Behind Doctor Reynolds stood a doctor with a clipboard; behind him, the inevitable nurse.

Harry shrugged. "It ain't easy."

Doctor Reynolds touched his shoulder. "I know, I'm sorry. Like I said, you don't need to decide today. But we'll have to know soon. She's been in ICU for a week. If you continue to prolong this, we'll have to move her."

"That won't be necessary. Today's the day. May I see her?"

The doctor smiled. "Of course."

They led Harry to her room and left him alone.

A sink, a countertop, a chair on wheels, a television mounted on the wall, a window overlooking the parking lot … the bed, the wheeze of machines, the puffing of the respirator, the beeping of her vitals, the drip of the IV.

*This is all you get: a bunch of stupid equipment. No procession of loved ones making their pilgrimage here. No flowers. No tears. Everyone you've ever known has abandoned you. Except me …*

God, she looked old. The operation had certainly aged her.

"Oh, Ma," he said. "This is how it ends, huh? This room, that window, those trees, that sun. Once you go, I go."

He searched her face for a reaction, but it was empty. Tubes going in, tubes going out. It seemed as if she were decaying, her body wrinkly and deflated.

Doctor Reynolds was right: time to let go.

*But I have to tell her first. She deserves to know.*

*No she doesn't. She deserves to rot—like all the others!*

Hansel again.

The creature didn't want her to know. It loved to hide in the shadows. But Harry was sick of hiding. For once he was going to drag everything out into the open.

He rubbed his face. "You're the only thing that kept me outta the loony bin, Ma. I doubt you real- ize that. You thought I came back from the army mentally sound, but that's not true. It changed me. I didn't return the same man."

He had lied to her, told her he'd tripped, broken his leg and was honorably discharged. But it was nothing that innocent. The truth involved claws, teeth, and hate—

—and a name:

*Hansel.*

He wanted to beat his head against the wall. He had to start with the day Hansel was born.

Harry sat in the chair beside her bed and took a breath.

"I hated everything about the army, Ma. The recruiters, the physical tests, the training. I did it because Dad had done it, and because I thought you wanted me to do it. They told me they would set me up as a MP. I'd have the best job on the base, they said, and be a person of power who could climb in rank.

"Bullshit. After boot camp they claimed I didn't pass the background check—because of the drug charges I incurred during high school. The only position open to me was mechanic. I know I told you I chose to be a mechanic, but I didn't. I wanted to be an MP."

He paused to gather his thoughts, not liking the beeping machines or the repetitious inflate/deflate of the respirator, nor the inhuman rise and fall of her chest.

Why was he confessing this to the husk of his mother? Did he think she was in there, listening?

No.

But he hoped.

"I was stationed at Fort Calendra in California when Desert Storm kicked off. But you already know that. Though I never told you what happened there, because you never asked.

"First I wanna tell you that they treated me like shit. I was a runt, an errand boy. I was a mechanic—yes, I spent a lot of time repairing jeeps and tanks returning from Iraq—but the rest of the time I was scrubbing latrines and washing dishes in the mess hall.

"I often wished they *would* ship me overseas so I could prove I was a soldier and not some scrawny screw-up.

"They used to torment us with rsome andom, sadistic shit. If they—*they* being any high-ranking sergeants—woke you at three a.m. asking you to shave your roommate's genitals, you did it. I once had to stand on a stool for eight hours, naked, with one foot in the air. And dammit, I did it, but I puked repeatedly into the bucket they placed at my feet.

"But you don't need to know all that. It was a horrible place. My roommate was a real creep. His name was Garrote. A weapons specialist, real crazy too. He was always fondling his rifle. He spent hours disassembling, cleaning, and reassembling rifles from Iraq. That was his job. He was muscular. Quiet. We never talked, never argued. He'd stay on his side of the room oiling a rifle or reading one of his survivalist tracts.

"I didn't get to know him, which was fine by me. He was weird anyway. I did hear some rumors about him, though. You're probably familiar with the "Don't Ask Don't Tell" policy, which stipulates that soldiers aren't supposed to talk about sexual orientation. Bullshit. If we knew that someone was queer, we talked about it, made jokes, even harassed them. But you had to be careful. If the queer told you'd get into trouble. You had to pretend to be nice and call him a fag and then laugh so he wouldn't know if you were serious. That's what we did with Garrote.

"I had two main friends at Calendra: Randy and Jay. Randy was an older guy, been there a while. Mechanic, like me. He'd served during Vietnam, had gone over to Iraq. Jay, on the other hand, was a young hotshot, always talking about going over so he could kill him some "sandniggers." So far hadn't, though.

"Each weekend we were granted temporary leave. We were allowed to take off from the base, hit the town to see our families. Or we could stay on and hang out with fellow soldiers in their apartments. Me, Randy and Jay often did this because none of us had any family in town. Jay had a girlfriend, but they always fought. Friday nights they'd come over and we'd get drunk and watch baseball. And we chose my apartment because Garrote left for the weekend. We often joked he was visiting his fag lover.

"One Friday he didn't leave and was there in his bed reading while we drank beer and watched my black-and-white TV on the counter. We ignored him until we got drunk. And then we started teasing him. Harmlessly at first, little gay jokes that I don't think he took offense at because he was smiling.

"'Hey Garrote, what's the biggest dick you ever took?' Then we'd all laugh. 'Hey, how'd you get to be queer, anyway? Did your daddy fuck you up the ass?' Laugh, laugh, laugh. It spread like wildfire. Before long we were trying to outdo each other while Garrote hid behind his book.

"I remember thinking, *What the hell, you big faggot, why don't you stand up for yourself?*"

Hansel was climbing his ribcage to his throat. He swallowed the creature back down.

His mother: pale, sunken eyes, the puff and wheeze of the respirator; mottled sunlight, sliced by the window shades, aimed upon her bed.

He had to tell her. After today he'd be gone and she'd be dead and there'd never be another opportunity.

"Things got worse."

The words hung in the air, written on the empty space above the hospital bed in puffy white letters. Memories rushed in like poison and the poison seeped into his brain.

"It's important you understand how drunk we were, Ma. We'd polished off two bottles of Jim Bean and a thirty pack of beer. I mean *real* drunk—blackout drunk. I can't remember who started it, but at some point we played a game like truth or dare, but just the darers. Fake ones at first. Jay dared Randy to sleep with his girlfriend, and of course Randy said yes. Laugh, laugh, laugh. Randy dared Jay to sleep with Sergeant Potters and we laughed again.

"But then things got disgusting. Randy put a cigarette out in his beer and drank it, then he puked in the kitchen sink. I had to lick Jay's feet. Jay had to gargle a mouthful of my piss I collected in a Styrofoam cup.

"God knows why. Like I said, it sorta spread like wildfire. This evil, childlike mischievousness. We weren't responsible adults anymore. We were kids who'd try anything once.

"The dares became sexual. Jay had to jerk-off into a cup and then drink it. I had to stick my nose up Randy's ass and take a big whiff. Randy had to cup my balls with his hand.

"Christ, why am I telling you this?

"Anyway, our attention finally landed on Garrote, who was pretending to sleep. Maybe he was asleep, but I sort of doubt it. Jay dared Randy to have sex

AARON J. FRENCH

with him—no, not sex ... *rape*. That's exactly what he said: *rape him*. Randy said only if I did it, and I said only if he did it. It was that simple. The three of us attacked him.

"He didn't submit willingly. He reached for the rifle beside his bed, though Randy knocked it from his hands. Garrote was bigger, and he tried fighting, but we overpowered him. Soon he stopped resisting and stared at the wall, his body jerking with the motions. I remember the sounds ... the blood running down his calves.

"I held his arms while the other guys did it, but when my turn came, something happened. My vision went black and I slipped away. I watched from outside my body. Watched as someone else raped this poor guy. It wasn't me laughing, Ma. It was Hansel."

Harry covered his face, not wanting to look at her.

"At that moment, the creature was born. It's another part of me, an evil part. It's like my *not*-self. Hansel. It's the one who did these bad things, not me.

"I'm not just one person, Ma, and that night in Calendra, I was Hansel. And after raping Garrote, Hansel beat him to a pulp with a beer bottle. Raped him with it. Jay and Randy were so freaked that they called the MPs. Garrote was rushed to the infirmary where he later died.

"The three of us were dishonorably discharged. Banished from the State of California. I wasn't brought up on charges. The military wanted to avoid an incident. At the time, a series of former army women had been coming forth with rape stories, and the military didn't want to exacerbate the problem. Garrote's family was fed some bullshit story about a training accident and was paid a considerable sum.

"That's how it started, Ma. That's how Hansel was born. From then, the creature has tried taking me over, but I've fought back.

"It does manage to get out and when It does people die. The creature loves children."

Harry removed his hands, checked to see if she was awake. He expected her to be. He expected her to leap out of bed and flee down the hospital corridor. Part of him *wanted* that to happen.

She was a carapace, a husk. Nothing inside, nothing out.

He was confessing to nothing, but it felt good.

"I've survived on my own ever since, but it was hard. When I moved to Arizona, I lived near a school; each time I walked to work I'd pass by it, see the children walking single-file, climbing the monkey bars, swinging, laughing, playing. Then a voice in my head would say, '*Ooh, I bet that one would be tasty. Pull his little pants down, slice him up wide.*'

"The voice frightened me because I didn't know whose it was. I thought I was the one having these terrible thoughts. It took me a long time to realize it was Hansel.

"I'd been out of the army a year when the creature got Its first taste of child. It was horrible, Ma, just like it was with Garrote. I was watching outside myself while Hansel hid in the bushes by the playground. Watched as It waited. Watched as It raped, stabbed, killed, and disposed of the body.

"There was nothing I could do and that drove me insane. I kept screaming 'Stop! Stop! You're crazy, don't do this!' but Hansel only laughed and pushed me into the prison of my mind.

"When I regained control of my body, I freaked. I sold what little I had, bought a car and fled Arizona the next day. I tried living in Albuquerque and for a while it went okay. I got a job busing tables, moved into a decent place. Met a girl.

"But the voice never quit. A terrible voice, always talking about rape and murder, blood and bones, and flesh. Showing me horrible images, giving me nightmares.

"I thought about seeing a psychiatrist, but I didn't have insurance and couldn't afford what the doctors charged. I decided to work at shutting the creature out myself. This was hard at first because I hadn't yet realized the creature was another person. I still thought It was me, and it's impossible to block out yourself. Only when I determined It was another self entirely did I have any success. Whenever Hansel showed me a gruesome sight, I'd shut my eyes and count. Sometimes I'd lock It in an imaginary room. This worked most of the time.

"Other times I'd have to listen to Its orgasmic rambling about killing some defenseless woman or young child. It would show me mental pictures of flayed bodies, and I would get sick and vomit.

"It always found a way out. In Albuquerque I watched while It raped and dismember two sixteen-year-old twin sisters. I even watched It cook and devour their flesh. I remember the terrified pleas of one as It chopped up the other ...

"And so I fled New Mexico, same as Arizona. A pattern soon developed: I'd run to a new place, take up residence, things would go smooth for a time, but then the creature would get out and kill again, and I'd be forced east. Unconsciously running to you.

"I thought about Garrote ... a lot. If only I had never participated, the creature would still be coiled in my stomach.

"I believe there's a monster abiding in everyone, waiting to get free, but It must be awoken—like it was for me. Then It never goes back to sleep—"

The door swung open and a nurse barged in.

Harry gulped back his sentence, took in a breath and tried to stop his hands from shaking.

Had she been listening?

He watched her perform her duties: checking the machines, glancing at various readouts, replacing the IV. She offered a smile. She was pretty in a plain sort of way.

*—rip—one, two, three—a fistful of hair. You know the sound it makes, you've heard it: like stepping on fortune cookies. And underneath ... ah, so sweet ...*

*Shut up!*

"Having trouble letting go?" she asked.

"Something like that."

She placed a redolent hand on his shoulder: lilacs, lotion, latex, antiseptic.

"That's the hardest part. But you just gotta remember: she's in a better place now where the world can't harm her."

He smiled and she gave him a pat on her way out.

*What does she know? I've been coming here every day for the past week and every day she says the same thing. I bet she thinks I'm a joke. I bet they all think that. A joke too weak to say those three magic words*—pull the plug …

*Wait for her*, the creature said. *In the parking lot. Then cut cut cut, saw saw saw, rip rip rip*—

*Shut up!*

There was a rustling from the bed and for a second he thought she was moving. He held his breath and waited.

Nothing.

Beeps and wheezes.

He sighed. Just a bit more to go before the darkness.

He continued his story.

"Eventually, I got all the way back to Brooklyn, all the way back to you. I remember that day. I was a wreck, had driven non-stop from Ohio where Hansel had butchered an entire family.

"You were so glad to see me. I remember the smile on your face. We had lunch at Fra Amiche's pizzeria. That was the best day I'd had in a long time. We had a pepperoni pie and a large pitcher of Pepsi and we sat by the window watching the cars go by. I told you that story about being honorably discharged. And I walked with a fake limp and pretended I was injured. I'm sorry I lied, Ma, but I was so ashamed.

"You brought me back to the Pierside Housing Projects in Canarsie, the place I grew up. You even gave me my old room, which was exactly how I'd left it. I got a job at the aquarium and helped with the bills and groceries. We spent those mornings strolling along the Canarsie Pier. Sometimes I went fishing.

"You told me after Dad died that you wanted nothing more to do with people. You cut yourself off from everyone—everyone except me because I was part of Dad. And that made me feel really special, Ma.

"I even started believing the creature had gone away. So much time passed that I thought I imagined the whole thing. The voices left me alone, the images went away. I thought of myself as being whole again.

"Out of nowhere, It was back with a vengeance. I was sitting in the courtyard of our building watching the neighborhood kids on the swing set when a voice said, *'That black kid in the sweater ... take him, pull back his flesh and drink his blood.'*

"I lost control of my body that day. Hansel took the poor kid behind the F building and bashed his brains in with a red cinder block. Left him there.

Then It came up to the apartment while you were taking a nap, and showered off, chucked the bloody clothes into the incinerator shoot. I didn't get my body back until later that night and I cried myself to sleep on my childhood pillow.

"It was Mrs. Wentertin's son from the L building. We were all devastated when they found the body. Some people claimed they saw me right before it happened and the police questioned me. I told them I didn't know anything. I told *you* I didn't know anything. But I was lying.

"Things returned to normal and I shut the creature out again. Years passed. Good years. It happened only one more time. Do you remember when the Peterburg girl went missing? That was Hansel. The creature raped her in the stairwell, strangled her, and then dumped her in a bush. It snuck out later that night and carried her body to the pier. Dumped her—"

Harry cried. The memories were too much.

His mother resembled a corpse with the tubes in her arm and another shoved down her throat. A living person's chest did not heave like that. She hadn't heard a word Harry said.

*She's in a better place now.*

He placed a hand on her clammy forehead and kissed her. Her lips were like sandpaper.

"Goodbye, Ma," he whispered.

He pressed the call button. Sat. Waited.

The same nurse arrived. She smiled at him.

"Yes?"

"I'm ready."

Her smile faded. She nodded, touched his shoulder and left the room. She came back with Doctor Reynolds and two orderlies.

"I'm ready," Harry repeated. "I've said my goodbye. You can turn her off."

The doctor nodded solemnly. He whispered to the nurse and she turned off the machines.

A cloud passed in front of the sun, casting shadows through the window. The room darkened.

Harry heard the tape peel away, the choke and gurgle as the nurse removed the respirator tube. The bed railing rattled.

"Don't you want—" he heard Doctor Reynolds say, but Harry was already in the hall.

The waiting room was empty.

The row of chairs, the nurses' station, the front lobby—all were vacant. The clock on the wall ticked. Something was moving, moving, moving … past everything, away from it all, exiting through the glass doors, getting loose. Free.

Grinning, the creature stepped out into the late afternoon.

# Sometimes They Hunt

## Chris Hertz

"It's climbing again."

Jesse Longabaugh gave the old man a sideways glance. "What's climbing?"

"The rain," said Butch. "The rain has all dried up."

Red soaked into his jeans.

Jesse gripped the wheel. "You're losing a lot of blood in my new truck."

Butch grinned as he whispered in childish singsong: "*The eency, weency spider climbing up the spout. Down came the rain and* washed *the spider out.*"

Butch flung his arms to emphasize the wash out and blood splashed across the glove box.

The old man laughed.

"That sombitch won't ever stop. He's patient. Yes, he is. So patient."

"Dammit, who are you talking about?"

Butch's eyes were glass. He sat hunched over, a wince of pain crinkling his face with the rhythm of a heartbeat, his left hand clamped to his right wrist. The hand was gone … a bloody stump inside a long-sleeved polyester button-down wrapped in a red and white bandana. His shirt was splotchy like a butcher's apron. Blood trickled onto his jeans with the slow drip of a leaky faucet, the kind you can't shut off.

*"Bright shone the sun to dry up all the rain. And the eency, weency spider climbed up the spout again."*

"Jesus," Jesse said. "He's off his nut."

The singing stopped.

"I ain't. I'm of sound mind. Just not body." He laughed again and lifted his stump for emphasis. "Yup, more rain, that's all. Like twenty years ago when it washed me out. But I keep climbing. Yes sir, I keep climbing. Like that spider."

Butch spent twenty years in State for molesting Jamie Longabaugh, Jesse's sister. Jesse wasn't sure why he had even pulled over the truck to help.

The old man was crackers, had lost too much blood and probably wouldn't make it to the hospital. Jesse tried to concentrate on the scenery. Black curtains draped over the world. The truck's headlights fanned out like snow from a plow, and melted in the darkness.

*"Out came the sun and dried up all the rain. And the eency, weency spider went out to hunt again!"*

Butch busted a gut as he finished.

"Those aren't even the words," Jesse said.

He sighed and eased off the accelerator as the truck curved around a dark bend. He loosened the top buttons on his shirt and ran his fingers through his hair.

Butch's face scrunched with pain.

For the first time, Jesse felt compassion.

"Hurts bad?"

Butch snorted.

"Well, what about your hand then?"

"My hand?"

"Your missing hand. You got it on ice? Maybe they can—"

"My hand's gone," Butch said, and then sang his deranged version of the song again.

Jesse's mind swirled. *Dump his old ass on the side of the road. No one will ever know. But, if you do, you'll miss a chance to reconcile the past.*

He drifted back twenty years: the courtroom, the judge slamming his gavel with a guilty verdict, the mixed emotions. Three kids with yellow hair: the smiling thirteen-year-old brother, the laughing twelve-year-old sister, and the youngest—nine— thoughtful, but still kind of above it all with a look that said he knew the truth but wouldn't admit it.

Shadows cloaked Butch's face. Jesse remembered a beaten man with slumped shoulders and a haggard appearance walking out of the courtroom, an old man even then. The bailiff had escorted him out in chains. Walking out, he had glanced back at the three kids. There was something in his eyes. Not fear, not anger, but something. Jesse could never

111

put his finger on it, not that he ever tried. But he was trying now.

What exactly does twenty years in prison do to a man?

Butch jumped in his seat. The wounded man winced. His paleness absorbed the red glow of the dash, turning him into a pink ghost. A shiver shook his frame.

Jesse switched off the air conditioner, cracked the windows.

"All right, listen," Butch said, his voice regaining some of its familiar timbre, "I don't know how much time we have."

"Hospital's about ten miles away, so probably about twenty minutes or so."

"I know how long it takes to get to the hospital. I'm talking about *time*."

Pain was thick on the old man's face. There was something else there too. Terror had gripped him for a second. This was a man who stood in front of a judge and accepted a twenty-year sentence for a crime he hadn't committed, not once showing a glint of fear, but now something had Butch Havren shaken up bad.

"Look," Jesse said, "if you're worried about your arm, I'll push it a little faster. But—"

"It ain't that. It's what I have to tell you. I can't promise you'll believe it."

"Try me."

"I think the bird started it."

"The bird?"

"The robin that committed suicide in my basement a couple weeks ago."

"Butch, what does that have to do with your hand?"

The old man didn't answer. Suddenly, he changed direction.

"You ever wonder how a spider catches a fly?"

"With a web."

"But the web don't move. The fly moves. So what makes a fly land on a web? Stupidity? Curiosity? The natural way of things?"

"Serendipity, I guess," Jesse answered.

"Serenwhadity?"

"Serendipity. It's like fate."

"Why don't you just say *fate*?" Butch's face turned as red as the dash. He seemed to gain strength as he spoke, as if he had forgotten about his hand. "You kids and your fifty-cent words. When are people gonna learn that two-cent words work fine. That's why the economy's in the crapper. All these people wasting money on expensive words, trying to sound smart. I got news for you, kid. I know you and I know your family. You ain't smarter than me and you ain't got the money for costly words. Or fancy cowboy hats and pickup trucks. If you wanna learn something, what I got to say is free. So shut up and listen. You owe me that much."

"Now hold on, Butch. I'm sorry for what my family did to you. I am. Jake and Jamie planned the whole thing—"

"I'm not talking about your brother and sister.

I'm talking about you. Think you're better than me? Well you ain't."

Jesse kept quiet.

"That's right," the old man said and grinned. "As I was saying, the spider and the fly ... the web don't move. The fly can pass by that web every day and never be in danger, until the one time it dives in, like committing suicide. That's what happened when the robin flew into my basement. Damned if it didn't commit suicide."

Jesse showed no reaction.

"I'd been out for a month. Spent that time at Deliverance, the halfway house in Mapleton. Couldn't *buy* a job. Not with *my* record. Long story short, the folks at Deliverance set me up with a job at the cemetery. Nobody wanted the job and no job wanted *me*, so I thought it was a good fit. The old caretaker was a bit of a hoarder. Part of the deal was I had to clean the mess left behind after his mysterious death. Two weeks of heavy lifting and the house was livable again. I had to contend with the storage room in the basement, but I took my time with it. I was standing there when a robin flew into the basement and landed on an old steel cage. It cocked its head, studying me, and jumped on my shoulder. Then for some reason it lifted off and went kamikaze straight into a hole in the floor. Burst through with a puff of feathers. But that wasn't the strange part. After the bird disappeared, I saw a solitary feather sticking out. If I'm lying, may I lose my other hand."

Butch raised a stump in the air as an oath and rivulets of red ran down his sleeve.

"The hole sucked in the feather like a kid slurping spaghetti."

Butch waited for a reaction, but Jesse didn't give him one. They were still a good seven miles from the hospital.

"I didn't know whether that hole led out to the cemetery or into the fiery pits of Hell. And I didn't care to find out neither, so I left it alone. Last weekend I was in the basement working on an old window air conditioner. Darla, my Yorkie, followed me to help."

"Darla?" Jesse found his voice. "The waitress at The Every Acre?"

"The two of us had a thing a while back."

"You have a Yorkie named after your ex-girl-friend?" Jesse laughed. "If you're not careful, Butch, folks will begin to think you have feelings. So, what happened?"

Butch looked quizzical.

"I mean, how'd you blow it with her?"

"I was sent to State for molesting a kid. Remember?"

Butch scratched at his stub.

"The AC sat on my workbench. I had unscrewed the motor when Darla growled. Something in the air she didn't like. It was sprawled on the dirt floor outside the hole ... a spider 'bout the size of my fist. Biggest dang spider I ever saw. It wasn't crawling. It was dead. Least it was lying upside-down. It was night-black and a hairy sucker.

I had to call Darla three times before she took her eyes off the thing and another three times before she went upstairs. I'd never seen her so riled. Hindsight being what it is, I should've known. Dogs sensing evil and all that. But I didn't know. How could I?"

Jesse passed on the rhetorical question.

"I grabbed the spade off the wall and stood over the spider, intent on ending its misery. But something stopped me. I don't have no special place in my heart for God's creatures, but I have to admit I was curious. Instead of slicing the spider in half, I scooped it up. Have you ever seen the underbelly of a spider?"

"Never had a reason," Jesse said.

"One of the creepiest things I ever seen. Looks like a hairy cootch, but the kind that could bite your head off."

Jesse cracked a smile.

"Pincers sharp as garden shears. I glanced at the steel cage, back to the spider, and suddenly the old caretaker's death wasn't a mystery anymore. I was Sherlock Holmes in my room, smoking a pipe and fiddling hot as the devil. One look at those pincers and I knew. The pet spider did it."

"Now hold on, Butch. Why would a pet kill its owner?"

"It's a spider, not a dog. Just because we keep things in cages, feed them, give them human names, call them pets, doesn't mean they love us or have any sense of loyalty. I've yet to meet a living creature—man or beast—that will thank you for caging it."

Butch shook his head.

"No, this spider was a killer. It was also still alive. Its legs twitched and there was a light behind its eight-ball black eyes. I opened the door to the cage and slid the spider in. Like a prison guard at the state pen, I swung the door shut. It latched and I shuddered. The sound of finality, a sound I'll always remember. The spider lay there, helpless. It was almost a pitiable thing and I admit feeling sorry for it. Locked up, lying on its back, hairy legs twitching ... Reminded me of Reggie."

"Who's Reggie?" Jesse asked.

"My first cell mate, a nervous sucker. Not cut out for life inside. Most aren't. He was bullied daily by one of the guards, but he never said a thing. Still, you could see the lava building behind his eyes. One day a guard bullied him one time too many and all that lava became an exploding volcano. Reggie went from fifteen years to death row. They fried him soon after. He didn't even care. The way he saw it, dead beat the hell out of locked up."

Butch offered a moment of silence.

"Just like Reggie my cell mate, Reggie the spider—as I began to call it—had had enough of that cage. When the rain keeps falling and washing you out, anger has a funny way of building. Like lava. One day you can't take it no more and Boom!"

Butch banged his stump against the dash to

accentuate the sound. Blood splattered across the cab. The old man should have doubled over in pain, but he seemed to take it in stride.

"The noise carried all the way upstairs. I ran to the basement. When I reached the store room, I found the cage on its side on the dirt floor. The top mangled. The cold steel bars jutted outward, leaving a gaping hole. The cage was empty except for the dried remnant of molted skin left behind by the former occupant—wispy and white like the ghost of a giant spider.

"The hole in the floor appeared double in size. I ran to the laundry tub and hooked the garden hose to the faucet. Stuffed the hose into the hole. Like an executioner pulling the lever, I turned the handle full blast. Down came the rain and washed that *mother* out. When I was satisfied, I stemmed the flow. But I forgot one important point. The spider never dies. It's patient. It waits. And when the sun comes out, it starts climbing again."

Butch paused, still searching for a reaction from Jesse.

"This week passed and I forgot all about it. I hadn't been in the basement since. I was busy with my cemetery duties. I wanted steak for dinner, so I stopped at the butcher and picked out a prime cut for me and a T-bone for Darla. When I walked in the house, I put the steaks on the counter and called for her, but she didn't come. She didn't bark or come running. The house was dead silent. And it was the *dead* part that worried me. I had a sick feeling—in that part of your gut where sick goes to fester—that Reggie had graduated from birds to dogs."

Butch rocked.

"I checked downstairs. Then the second floor. I was avoiding the basement, but I knew that's where I'd find Darla, or whatever was left of her. I flicked on the light above the cellar steps. When I hit the basement floor, it was like stepping into a cloud. A fine gray mist hung from the ceiling. The air was dry. It didn't take a rocket scientist to know it wasn't mist at all, but webbing.

"I moved carefully—avoiding contact with the silky strands. I'd seen enough nature shows to know *that* was a bad idea. Don't get me wrong. I wasn't scared. Not of the web. Not of Reggie. Not of finding Darla's body. Until I saw the mound of molted spider skin covering the workbench. That's when self-preservation kicked in and I decided to beat feet. But fear wrapped its icy claws around my heart and squeezed. Feet can't run fast enough from that kind of terror."

The rocking intensified.

"I must've flown from the bench to the foot of the stairs. That's where I found Darla hanging upside-down from the ceiling, wrapped in a silken shroud. I hadn't noticed her before. She was stone dead. My natural reaction was to yank her down, so I did, and my hand caught in the webbing. Like ringing a dinner bell …

"Reggie's hairy legs were on me in an instant.

Six-foot tall if he was an inch. The eency weency spider all grown up. His course black hairs were now parted by angry red stripes. Branded by his prison cell. I pitched forward onto the steps and Reggie lunged at my head, pincers clicking, mouth drooling. I lifted my hand—the one still stuck to the dog—to shield my face. The fangs sunk into Darla's dead flesh and when they ripped away, I heard a sound like a tree limb snapping. I knew what had happened. I jammed the bloody stump against my chest, bounded the stairs and out into the yard. That's when you happened to drive by."

Butch took a deep breath as his story ended, his ruined hand folded over the other as if in prayer. The dark shadows of trees and shrubs had given way to rocky hills. The smoky orange glow of the town lights ignited like a dull flame above the horizon. They were still over three miles away, but getting closer.

Jesse stared out of the windshield, face bunched with confusion. For a moment, the only sound was a humming of the tires on blacktop.

And then Jesse burst out laughing.

Butch's eyes bulged and his face turned green. He was either in severe pain, or Jesse had pushed the old coot too far.

"Pull over," Butch said.

"What? Why? Come on, you don't expect me to believe—"

"If you don't want a mess in your truck, you best get off to the side here. Now."

Jesse pulled onto the shoulder. He lowered the passenger window from his control on the driver side and Butch wretched out the window.

A loud thud filled the cab as if something heavy had crashed on top of the truck. Butch seemed to sense what was happening. He ducked into the cab and raised the window as a shadow flashed by—at least Jesse *thought* he saw a shadow.

The old man's lips were colorless, eyes sunken, cheeks more pallid than when he had first stepped into the truck back at the cemetery. Jesse thought he might pass out. Butch wavered a moment and then reached out his good hand—blood dripping across the cab—and grabbed Jesse's shoulder. He tried to speak, but managed gibberish.

"My hand ... got a taste now ... lost patience ..."

Jesse reached for the door.

The sanguineous hand squeezed his shoulder. Blood soaked into the fabric of Jesse's shirt, leaving a violet stain.

"Don't you see?" Butch said. "There's nothing as sinister as the patience of a spider. No matter how many times it's washed out, it will keep climbing that damn drain pipe. Or it will sit on its web for days as still as a statue, and wait. It's hungry, sure. It needs food, but it also knows if it's patient, food will arrive like manna from heaven. It's bone chilling when you think about it. But even spiders can lose patience. What most people don't know about spiders is that sometimes, when they get a taste for a certain meal, they leave the web. Sometimes they hunt."

"Enough." Jesse shook off the gore-covered hand. "I don't know what you're talking about and I don't care. I'm going to see what hit my truck."

He opened the door and stepped out.

The old man fell onto the driver's seat, splattering blood across the cab.

"It's suicide," Butch said. "Don't you understand?"

Jesse grabbed the old man's collar. "Don't *you* understand? You laid it on a little too thick. I'm not nine years old anymore."

Butch's face filled with resentment. It was the same look he gave when he was escorted out of the courtroom all those years ago. For a moment, Jesse was nine again: the bailiff leading Butch away, the prisoner turning to his accusers.

He put a hand to his face and tore the memory away like a mask, but instead of two eye sockets there were eight, and instead of teeth there were pincers as sharp as garden shears.

The vision shook Jesse and for a moment he thought Butch might lunge at him. Instead, the old man's black eyes rolled white and he slipped out of consciousness.

Jesse pulled a long-handled flashlight from behind the driver's seat and shut the door behind him.

A solid beam burst onto the pavement. He checked the roof, the chrome top glistening. Not a dent or scratch. Had he imagined the noise? The high beams illuminated the horizon. Nothing.

The bedliner was nicked-up a bit, but nothing was there either. When Jesse's boots hit the pavement, he heard it. On the other side of the truck. A low clicking noise followed by a scratching sound. Something crawling along the pavement to the back bumper.

He angled the flashlight behind the truck and there it was, crouching behind the tailgate. It was six feet tall if it was an inch, covered in bristly black hair, fangs clicking, mouth drooling, eight-ball black eyes lifeless except for the volcano of fire burning behind them, angry red scars branded into the abdomen like prison bars.

*(What exactly does twenty years in prison do to a man?)*

"I'll be a sonofa—"

Jesse ran the flashlight across the figure.

Butch stood outside the truck, his chest heaving and body shaking. His eyes darted around until they found Jesse in a chalk-outline pose on the pavement. He spat blood and chuckled at the sight. Softly at first, and then louder in great belly guffaws, the kind that leave you paralyzed and gasping for air. He kicked his heels in a deranged jig and sang into the night:

*"And the eency weency spider went out to hunt again!"*

Butch danced and laughed and sang and slipped his fake stub hand—whole and intact—out from his sleeve. He dropped the plastic bag the butcher had filled with calf's blood.

"Sometimes they use bait," Butch said as he

waltzed behind the truck.

Eight smiling eyes greeted him like a puppy greeting its master. Eight hairy legs rested on their haunches, the striped abdomen wagging gently. Six feet tall if it was an inch.

"Not so eency weency, are we?"

Butch patted the hairy forehead, carefully avoiding the swollen, dripping fangs. "Cage a creature and you make an enemy. Set them free and you've made a friend for life."

The spider clicked its pincers.

Butch indicated Jesse's body. "That ought to hold you over until we visit Jake Longabaugh."

Crimson flecks flew from the poisonous tips.

Butch smiled wide. "I know. I can't wait either. But, for now, let's go home. You've had a big night. This time you can ride up front."

The old man wrapped one arm around Reggie's hairy shoulder and pointed the other toward the horizon.

"We'll climb that big, bad spout together, you and I," he said as they strolled to the truck. "I ain't worried about no rain, neither. Not with you riding shotgun."

# Sizzle

## Weldon Burge

"He wants brain surgery?"

Chambers opened the folder that his receptionist gave him and glanced over the file.

"He wants you to 'cut the sizzle' out of his brain," she said. "This one's a basket case, Larry. Martin Pleasanton, straight from the hills of West Virginia. He complained of a burning sensation on the back of his head, but all I found was a slight inflammation where he had been scratching. Guy gave me the willies."

"Is this all you got out of him?"

"He wouldn't talk. Said I'm one of *them* and couldn't be trusted. He refused to answer any more questions."

Chambers removed his glasses and pinched the bridge of his nose. A cluster migraine lurked behind his right eye like a clawing malignancy.

"How does he know *I'm* not one of them," he said, "whoever the hell *they* are?"

She threw up her hands. "Looneytoons, if you ask me."

"Well, send him in. Then you can go on home. I don't think I'll be long with Mr. Pleasanton."

"Oh, nearly forgot. Your wife is on hold. Send her through?"

"Damn. I wonder what she wants." Chambers sighed. "Yes."

"One other thing. Hold your nose. This guy apparently isn't familiar with indoor plumbing."

Chambers put on his glasses, not wanting to miss her curvaceous departure. He was amazed at how much pliable, willing flesh could be poured into her tight dress. "We're still on for tomorrow night?"

"Wouldn't miss it." She smiled like a fifteen-year-old coquette, and then left the room.

When the call buzzed through, he lifted the receiver. Before he could even say hello—

"I won't be here when you get home, you sorry sonofabitch!"

Chambers' headache suddenly intensified. "It's not what you think, Joanna."

"Not what I think? I want the bitch fired. Terminated. Dead."

A grizzled old man entered the room. Chambers, with a hand gesture, offered him the seat in front of his desk.

"Listen, Joanna." His voice was calm, reasonable. "I have one more patient, a new one. Wait for me. I'll be home in an hour or so and then we'll straighten this mess out. It really isn't what you think."

There was a long pause.

Dial tone raked into his ear.

"Trouble with the missus?" the old man said.

"Something like that."

After the usual amenities, Chambers balefully looked at the chunk of questionable humanity seated across the desk; Pleasanton embodied all that was least desirable about being in the medical profession.

Chambers forced a Hippocratic smile.

According to the scant information Pleasanton offered Miss Lambert, he was sixty-four. His sun-baked, saurian skin suggested greater antiquity. His appearance inspired no hope for an intelligent conversation. The man's teeth were black at the gums, scraps of God-knows-what rotting between them.

Although Chambers knew little about fashion, he knew a pile of filthy laundry when he saw one. The man smelled of urine.

"So, Mr. Pleasanton, you're from Haskenville," Chambers said. He pretended to study the file on his desk.

"No, not precisely." Pleasanton's voice was as gruff as his appearance. He scratched the back of his head. "Don't own no car. Had to walk all the way to Haskenville to catch the dangburn bus. Must be a ten mile walk. Seemed like thirty. Don't get out much, I guess. Never been to no doctor, neither."

"And you're a widower, Mr. Pleasanton?"

"Marty. All my friends call me Marty."

"Okay. Marty."

"My wife had an accident." He sighed and continued to scratch the back of his head. "Bad. Real bad. Messy. She died quick, God bless her."

"Sorry to hear that."

Pleasanton grimaced. His fingers tightened around something at the base of his skull.

"They did it. They always make me do things."

"They?"

Chambers looked at his watch. Looneytoons was right.

"I'll get to that." Pleasanton pulled something from his thick, gray hair. He opened his hand and, finding it empty, frowned. "I'm pretty content livin' alone in the mountains. Up there with my goats, pigs, and chickens. And dogs. Got about twenty dogs. All got the mange. So, I suppose I ain't alone. Just don't have much use for folk. Specially city folk." Pleasanton's eyes were dull, unfocused and bloodshot.

Chambers closed the manila folder. He wanted the old fart out of his office, but he didn't want a future malpractice suit either. It just required patience and some degree of acting ability.

"Tell me about this discomfort in your head, Mr. Pleasanton."

"Marty. Call me Marty." The old man pulled his chair closer to the desk, as if to impart a secret. "It all started last fall when I was pullin' turnips and rutabagers. Felt this bug crawlin' up my neck, right back here."

He reached behind his head to part his greasy hair, revealing large yellow stains under his arms.

"I thought it was one of them big grasshoppers. But it weren't no grasshopper. Then, I heard the sizzle in my head. Not loud at first. A little sizzle, like bacon in my brain. Then the voices started. Evil voices tellin' me what to do and what nasty things *they'll* do if I don't do as they say."

*Acute paranoia*, Chambers thought. *Delusions of persecution. Schizophrenia.*

"Who do you think they are?"

"I ask them, but they don't answer. Just laugh." He seemed to deep-dredge for a thought.

Chambers leaned back in his chair. He mentally listed some psychologists.

"Where do you think they come from, these things in your head?"

Pleasanton smiled, displaying molars blackened by age and neglect.

Chambers couldn't stand to look at him.

"What do these things want, Marty?"

"My brain. Don't you see? They told me they started with pigs and dogs and such. Simple animals. Controlin' their brains. Now they want to control my brain. I won't let 'em, and they don't like that much. No sir."

"And that's why you came to me?"

"Doctors cut cancer and other bad things out of people. A doctor sliced a rotten appendix out of my sister. She died though. Gangrene. Lord, musta been thirty years ago. Anyway, I want you to cut the sizzle out of me."

Chambers leaned forward, ignoring the man's overwhelming stench.

*Insanity wears many masks.*

"I honestly don't think I can help you, Marty. I'm not a surgeon, for one thing. I'm a general practitioner. It's not an organic problem." He noticed doubt and confusion clouding Pleasanton's eyes, so he added, "but I do know someone who can help. An associate of mine."

"Associate?"

"A psychologist. I think if you talk with him, he can—"

He glared at Chambers. "You think I'm crazy."

"No, Marty. I'm—"

"Don't call me Marty!" His lips receded, baring his teeth like a trapped cur. His brow tightened. "You ain't no friend of mine. You one of them, ain't ya? You want to hurt me."

"No," Chamber said, his voice calm. "I'm here to help."

"Liar!"

The old man's face contorted. His eyes bulged and he fell back into the chair, hands grasping desperately at empty air. He gurgled in a mockery of a scream. His tongue stretched from the moist cavern of his mouth like a thick, purple worm.

Thinking the man was having an epileptic seizure, Chambers bolted around the desk.

Spasms ripped through Pleasanton's body. His head wrenched forward. There was a sound like an over-ripe melon splitting. The man shuddered, and then pitched face-down on the desk as rancid smoke curled from a charred hole in the back of his head.

Chambers pressed Pleasanton's wrist, but could not find a pulse.

He examined the smoldering wound.

Bone protruded from the blackened brain tissue within. Then Chambers felt something crawling in his hair.

"My God!"

His fingers tore frantically at his scalp, but nothing was there.

An invisible, searing blade pierced the base of his skull. Pain flashed through his head like lightning.

Chambers screamed as agony crumpled him to his knees beside the desk.

*Sizzling.*

Chambers raised his head. The pain was gone.

*Hi, doc,* a malicious, high-pitched voice whispered in his ear. *The old geezer wasn't what we wanted anyway. Not very bright. We think you're our boy. First thing we want you to do is kill your wife. You'll enjoy that, won't you? Then, we have plans. Lots of plans.*

Chambers stood, stretched his neck, and then slowly looked around the room as if taking everything in for the first time.

The voice was right. There were quite a number

of things he'd been meaning to do. All he needed was a little encouragement.

Almost absentmindedly, Chambers grabbed what used to be Martin Pleasanton by the collar and dragged him to the large closet at the back of his office. Something soft and pleasant prickled the base of his skull.

He smiled, remembering the package of bacon in the refrigerator at home. He made a mental note to fry some of it later—if time allowed after his fun and games with Joanna.

# I Wanted Black

## Michael Bailey

The crimson balloon pushed through the surface of the puddle with viscous liquid that resembled oil rolling off the glossy rubber. A series of prismatic rings reached out and I heard my father's voice calling for me, silently, as if the balloon was inflating with his last breath and he was trying to say my name but couldn't; like his voice had died years ago, the air from his lungs still trapped inside, pushing the mess of oil on the ground toward me instead.

*David*, he tried to say.

This wasn't a lucid dream. I thought that too, at first. Lucidity is just a word fabricated for all the people in the world who think the strange things happening around them cannot possibly be real.

*David*, the balloon tried to say.

It inflated further and spun. A white piece of twine trailed beneath it, pulled taut into the water as if someone below were holding it down.

I reached for the twine and it was like plucking a guitar string. There was definitely something down there, tethering the balloon in place.

*Dad,* I said. *It's time to let go. You died when I was seven.* But I knew it was me who needed to let go.

It happened on my birthday. All my friends were there. There were red balloons everywhere: tied onto the backs of the chairs in the dining room, hanging from fan blades, kids running around with them anchored to their wrists, popped ones on the carpet like mottled blood spots. I don't know why my mother chose red. It wasn't my favorite color. My favorite color at the time was black, but she always told me black wasn't a color, it was the absence of color; so I guess she had decided on a real color for me.

*I wanted black, Dad,* I told the balloon.

The oily substance dripping from the balloon was black and so was the puddle. I touched the balloon and the surface was slick and smelled sweet. Like a kid, I brought my finger to my mouth and tasted it. I don't know why. The flavor reminded me of butter frosting and made me think of the cake.

*(Blow out the candles, David)*

I counted the candles twice to make sure I was seven. All of my friends stood around me in a semicircle, my mother behind me wielding a spatula and knife. She held them skyward with her elbows tucked against her waist. She looked at me like I was her puppy, her head tilted to the side, a wide smile and sparkly teeth.

*(Blow them out, David)*

My father wasn't home yet. He was supposed to be home by three when the party started. I remember him leaving a few hours earlier and I was mad because he had lied to me. He told me he had to work. He never worked weekends. I knew he was lying because he smiled. There's no way you can look your son in the face and lie to him on his birthday without smiling.

He told me once that the littlest things you do in life impact those around you in ways you may never know, so it is for this reason that everything you do should be backed with love. I was thinking of that when I finally made my wish. I blew out six. The seventh almost went out. It was the sole red one in the mix and it flickered back to life, killing my dreams. I was doing the little things—blowing out a rainbow assortment of cheap candles, wishing for my father to be home. Backed with love.

Wishes only come true if you blow them all out. I remember wax melting onto the butter frosting, red bleeding pink against the white. A part of me hoped that if the flame could flicker back to life, it might flicker back to death. It mocked me. Like the balloons. I wanted to let it burn all the way out, thinking my wish still had a chance if the flame died on its own. And then my mom leaned over my shoulder and blew it out.

That was a long time ago.

The crimson balloon no longer inflated. The oily substance ran the length of the twine to the puddle below. My reflection was concealed somewhere on its surface, the way words hide on paper until you let them out with ink. If I let myself out, the puddle would reveal a seven year old boy crying onto his birthday cake.

*David*, he tried to say.

I didn't want to think about the party, but there it was again.


Someone had knocked on the door and I thought it was him. I knew he had lied about having to go into work and so I thought it might be him returning from the store with a last-minute present. With tears running the course of my red balloon cheeks, I ran to the door.

*(Is your mother home?)*

A police officer.

*(Yes)*

My mother, behind me, a hand on my shoulder.

*(There's been an accident)*

The last thing he ever gave me ...

*It's time to let go, David.*

He died instantly, the officer told my mother. No pain. I guess it doesn't hurt much to have a car cross the center divider and hit you head-on at freeway speeds. It doesn't hurt to have a steering column pass through your chest. It doesn't hurt to have the lower half of your body severed by an engine block.

It was my birthday and my dad was dead.

*David*, the balloon tried to say.

I fell to my knees, ran my fingers along the twine. I followed it to the surface of the puddle and let my hand pass through the greasy liquid. It was hot, like blood, and sickly sweet. It coated my hand, my wrist, and then my forearm. I couldn't help but taste it as my lips made contact. My entire arm emerged to find what was holding the balloon in place.

And then I found what I was looking for. The twine was tied around my father's wrist just like the kids at my party.

*I don't want them anymore, Dad.*

His hand wrapped around mine and squeezed.

*Why did you have to lie to me? Why did you go back?*

After the accident, police found a portable helium tank and a bag of black balloons in the trunk. He had gone back because I had wanted black. Not red.

The last thing he ever tried to give me was his love.

*I don't want them anymore.*

The hand beneath the surface let go.

*No!*

Crazily, I reached for him, his fingers falling away … reaching for me, but falling away. They were too slick and I couldn't hold on. He sank, pulling the twine and the balloon with him. I wrapped my fingers around the twine, but he was too heavy and it slipped through my grasp. The balloon dipped into the oily black puddle and I could finally grab hold of the base.

Stretching tight, it said goodbye with the last of my father's breath.

*David*, the balloon tried to say.

The twine broke.

The crimson balloon soared to the sun.

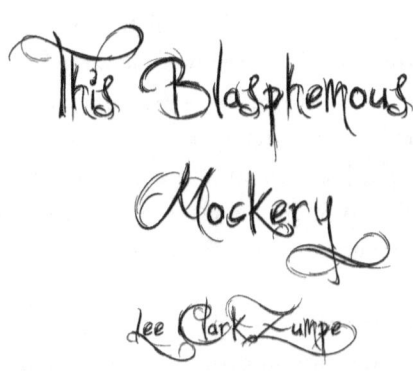

# This Blasphemous Mockery

Lee Clark Zumpe

Joe had learned to detest his nightly ride beneath the streets of New York, a tradition that had lasted eleven years. The way the metal serpent slithered below the ground repulsed him. Some nights he spent the journey staring out the window beyond his faint reflection. The thin membrane of concrete had worn so thin in a few places that he could see the goings-on of Hell on the other side of the façade, and a host of eager demons.

All the disguises seemed to be deteriorating as the guillotine edge of the coming apocalypse drew to a close. Sometimes he saw Dark Gods squirming in the shadowy alleyways taunting homeless drunkards. He heard wicked whispers billowing out of sewer drains and saw indescribable things shuffling across the rooftops of tenement buildings by night.

Long ago, he thought he might be losing his mind, fearing that he alone was the target of their malfeasance. Elizabeth, his wife, insisted he seek professional help. Stretched out on an uncomfortable sofa, Joe recounted the ghastly visions to a psychotherapist. By the close of the two hours, he was convinced the psychotherapist was one of them.

Shortly afterward, they took Elizabeth away. The action did not surprise him. He saw her go. It appeared mundane to the uneducated onlooker. She seemed to leave willingly with her arm wrapped about some tall fellow in an expensive three-piece. Joe knew better. He saw the man's tail curled in his trousers, the facial tentacles writhing below the artificial layer of flesh, and could smell the demon's repugnant breath.

*Who dares insult us with this blasphemous mockery*, he had whispered to himself as the thing escorted her to some hellish condemnation.

Joe mourned her disappearance for months, even contemplated suicide. But in the end, he recognized his duty to society. Joe was one of the few who could see beyond the subterfuge. The demons had much larger objectives than torturing him: they had begun some kind of incursion, an invasion. He could not sit idly and let them conquer New York City.

As the subway shuddered to a stop, Joe eyed the

other passengers. Expressionless toilers, innocent and ignorant, milled dazedly about the car. Wrinkles crept along their flesh. The bones became brittle. Errant proteins tunneled through their grey matter. Worries over money, relationships, religion and life so consumed them, they could not see the horrors around every corner. They were blind.

Joe waddled up the staircase, welcoming the embrace of a street lamp. He found the sidewalk barren and tried his best to avoid the island of shadows that huddled at the mouth of each alley. He clung tenaciously to his briefcase and shuffled his feet over the cement, anxious to reach the comfort of his apartment.

"Don't make a sound," a deep voice commanded.

Something cold and sharp dug into the small of his back. Hands like claws clamped onto his shoulders and dragged him away from the light and into the shadows.

"We'll make this real quick, real quiet and real painless, okay?"

"Who—?" Joe said, but already knew the answer.

"Drop the briefcase and turn around real slow."

Joe did as instructed. The briefcase splashed into a murky puddle. The back streets always seemed plagued by inexplicable tarns—watering holes for the rodent population.

The blade of a butterfly knife glimmered light from a distant street lamp.

"I don't want to have to kill you, man," said a young man in a trench coat. "Just gimme your wallet and watch, and you can go on home."

Joe saw the double row of jagged bloodstained teeth, the black-on-black eyes blinking sideways, the thin viper tongue dancing in the deep chasm of its mouth.

In one swift, graceful move, Joe forced the blade from the demon's hand and broke its arm. Tears bubbled to its eyes. He dragged the demon into the belly of the alley. He kicked it in the chest several times, broke a few ribs, and then threw it to the ground between some garbage cans. Its paws waved, begging for mercy.

"Don't hurt me, man … please."

Joe shrugged and stomped on its windpipe. Then he went to work as the thing's facial tentacles whipped about frantically. A hundred eyes stared skyward from its true face as he cut and peeled the fake one away.

Joe neatly wrapped a handkerchief around his prize, glanced around the alley, retrieved his brief-case from the puddle, and headed home.

His cat sped across the living room floor and brushed against his legs.

"Just a minute, Daisy," Joe said, tossing the brief-case to the floor.

He flipped a switch on the wall and an oscillating fan purred as light sent darkness scurrying. From his pocket he removed the damp, crimson-tinged handkerchief and held it out delicately. He opened the chest freezer at the foot of his bed, which contained his collection of masks. He would soon need a larger freezer.

The cat jumped onto the rim and enjoyed the cool air spilling from the icebox. She sniffed the blood and hissed.

"It's okay, Daisy." He tossed the kerchief and its contents onto the pile. "Just another face in the crowd."

# Gasoline

## S.C. Hayden

Sparks of light winked like fireflies in the periphery of Steven's vision, if it was vision; everything else was a strange fuzzy gray. He smelled gasoline.

*I must have been in a car accident.*

There was a warbling *whop whop whop* of a giant fan or helicopter.

*Maybe I'm being airlifted to a hospital.*

He had a vague memory of driving on the highway in the rain. He was sure he could figure it out if he could focus his thoughts, but they fell away as quickly as they formed. He tried to piece it all together.

Steven hung a clear plastic bag filled with deep red liquid from an IV pole. "This is blood, Mr. Detrolio. You lost a lot of blood. That's probably why you feel so winded."

An old man stared at him from a hospital bed.

"Your blood carries oxygen to the cells—"

"I don't need a goddamn science lesson," the old man said, "just do what you have to do."

"Come on, Dad," a woman said, placing her hand on Steven's shoulder. "He's trying to help you." Before she removed her hand, she squeezed gently, massaging Steven's shoulder with her thumb for a half-second too long.

"Bahh," the old man grumbled.

Mr. Detrolio was seventy-eight, which put the woman in her early fifties, although she looked much younger. She wasn't wearing a wedding ring, but several rings sparkled on her fingers. If she was alone, she didn't suffer for it, at least not financially. Trashy-sophistication and money.

When Steven finished hanging the blood, she followed him out of the room and stopped him in the hallway.

"I know he can be a handful," she said, "but he's a sweet man, and he's all I have left. He doesn't mean to be so nasty."

"I know he doesn't, and he's no trouble at all. It's tough for a man his age to cope with the loss of independence," Steven said, quoting verbatim from his nursing ethics textbook.

"You're so *good*," she said, folding his hand in hers. "You're *too* good."

She pulled his hand to her stomach.

He felt warmth through her shirt.

"I'm going to give you my phone number. I want

you to call me if anything happens, anything at all."

She trailed her fingers across his open palm.

"In fact, you can call me anytime you want. I think we could do a lot for each other."

Steven watched her go, listening to the *clip clop* of high heels on the linoleum.

For as long as Steven could remember, he'd been attracted to older women. He was definitely not the type you'd find eyeballing young girls at shopping malls. Women his own age—even the older thirty-something's—looked like frustrated mannequins. He blamed television. The sexual *ideal* was neurotic and anorexic.

Older women had a certain strength, a kind of been-there-done-that confidence he found sexy. He liked crow's feet and laugh lines. He liked the stern capability he saw in their eyes. He liked to read the histories in their bodies: the half-moon scar of an appendectomy, the silvery stretch marks of motherhood, the weathered flesh. Things that spoke of character.

Steven was exactly what an older woman was looking for: an attractive younger man without baggage or attachment, happy to please and to learn, and when it was over, willing to move on without drama or spite.

Eventually the weekend was upon him and he found himself toying with the cell phone in his pocket. He pulled the wrinkled yellow paper from his wallet and smoothed it open in his palm. The name Adriana was scrawled in looping script.

Steven dialed the numbers, enjoying the fleeting sensation of free-fall that came with groping into the unknown.

He imagined her wrapped in a towel, hair wet.

"I knew you'd call. My father's fine. He's recovering well. I just spoke to him a half-hour ago. I know that you're not at the hospital because I asked for you. Does that mean you're calling to take me out?"

Steven admired the way she took control of the conversation.

"I wanted to see how you were doing. You seemed flustered earlier. I was just—"

"If you want to *see* how I'm doing, you'll pick me up at ten o'clock and you'll take me out for a drink. It's a gorgeous night and I'm going stir-crazy in this apartment."

"Well, what can I say to that?"

"You can say 'I'll be there at ten.'"

"I'll be there at ten."

"There's a good boy."

She gave him an address in East Boston on the hill near the statue of the Madonna. Steven knew the hill well; he'd gone there with his father as a kid to watch the planes land. The old houses tucked into its slopes once looked out upon a beautiful working-class Italian neighborhood before immanent domain cleared it to make room for Logan Airport.

Steven showered, dressed and thought about where he would take her: someplace quiet, not too brightly lit; someplace where they wouldn't have to talk over loud music. He was excited racing though the night in a light rain to an encounter with a woman he didn't know, an encounter that would most certainly lead to sex.

*Is that it? Is that what happened? I was driving to that woman's house, driving in the rain and speeding.* He must have crashed his car. He imagined himself lying in the twisted wreckage, blind and dying.

But there was more.

He'd taken an East Boston exit and navigated the neighborhood's narrow, winding streets. She lived in a small apartment building at the base of the hill. He buzzed the number she'd given him on the intercom.

"Hello," she said in the same breezy way she'd answered the phone.

"It's me," he answered.

The lobby door unlocked.

Steven stepped out of the elevator onto the fourth floor and knocked on her door. It swung open and she was dressed in dark blue silk pajamas with white piping. Her hair was thrown over her shoulders and her feet were bare.

"I thought I'd save you the trouble of taking me out for a drink." She motioned him inside. There was a bottle of scotch on the coffee table, two glasses and a small pail of ice.

The apartment was attractive, but it had a feel

of cool sterility. The lights were too bright and the white wall-to-wall carpeting and plush white sofa seemed to increase the glare. A freestanding bookcase in one corner of the room housed floral pattern porcelain plates; a second in the adjacent corner held miniature porcelain clowns and a blue vase filled with pastel paper flowers.

It wasn't the sort of room you'd call a den, or even a living room for that matter. It was a single woman's apartment, but more than that it was the home of a neurotic tidier. The glass top on the coffee table looked as though human hands had never touched it. The air had a motionless, disinfected quality.

Steven felt like he was back at the hospital.

"I'll pour us some drinks," she said, smiling. She sat on the big couch and patted the space beside her.

Steven absentmindedly brushed the seat of his pants with his hands before sitting.

"A drink would be nice. Your apartment is beautiful."

"It feels like a prison."

She looked odd sitting in her pajamas with her hair brushed out over her shoulders, as though she were pretending to be a little girl at a sleepover. He imagined a stuffed animal or two on her bed. She turned to him, her knees touching his, and placed a hand on his thigh. Steven stiffened and was suddenly aware of her perfume.

"What kind of drink do you want, Kenny?"

He smiled at that, *Kenny*. Had she already forgotten his name? He slid his hand over her thigh, immediately bold.

*I'm going to take what I want here and she wants me to take it.*

"My name's Steven," he whispered, bringing himself closer.

Suddenly, they were kissing. The silk under his hand warmed as he traced her inner thigh. When he reached her crotch, her pajamas were damp.

"Come with me," she said.

She led him into a dimly lit bedroom and crawled across the bed. Half-open blinds threw a surreal striped pattern over her body. There were no stuffed animals, but the dresser was adorned with more porcelain figurines, clowns, and prancing ponies.

Soon she was underneath him, squirming and moaning. Steven rolled a condom in place, but she stopped him before penetration.

"Wait," she said, breathing heavily. "Do you have to do this?"

What the fuck was this? Was she going to leave him with his dick in his hand after she'd just soaked through her pajamas? It was all part of the thrill of going home with strangers. You never knew what to expect, never knew how crazy a person might be until you were immersed in their element.

She cupped his testicles.

"Do you really need to do that to me?" she said in a soft child-like voice. "Are you so frustrated that you have to fuck me?"

He was so thrown off by the sudden change that he was unsure how to respond. What was with the singsong voice? Was she into role-playing? Did she want him to talk dirty?

"Listen, if you don't want to do this, we can stop. I thought—"

"I know, baby, it must be awful for you," she interrupted. "I'm going to help you. Just stay here and relax."

She left him alone in the bedroom for several minutes. When she returned, she was carrying white towels and a glass bowl filled with soapy water and a large sponge.

She knelt on the bed beside him and spread the towels out over his stomach and thighs.

"Relax baby, just relax," she whispered, pulling off the condom. She wet her hand in the bowl and stroked him. "Here come all the pretty, pretty girls."

She rung the sponge in the bowl and wiped his erection before taking it in her mouth. She alternated between falating him and stroking him with her hand. When he wasn't in her mouth, she sang softly, "Here come all the pretty girls, the pretty girls are coming."

He came in her mouth and she swallowed.

"I know you feel better now," she said, cleaning him off.

He had no idea what to say. They dressed in the half-light of the bedroom and he watched her pull the silk pajama bottoms up and over her ass. Her body was surprisingly tone and well-proportioned. She had aged fantastically and probably knew it. He had an unexpected surge of desire and wanted her again. This time he wanted to take her fully. None of this weird washing and singing. Just lay her down and fuck her properly, but when he advanced, she was cold and rigid. It was over. She walked him to the oversized white couch and they sat.

This was always the tricky part—extricating yourself from the situation, or staying the night. There was no chance he was staying, even if he still wanted to fuck her. She was strange, and the apartment cold and uninviting. The porcelain clowns were unsettling and he still wanted a drink. But not here, not with her. He could stay, make some small-talk and then say something about having to work in the morning. She wouldn't be surprised. She'd done this before.

And then she buried her face in her hands and sobbed.

*Fuck.*

"What's the matter?" he asked.

"Oh god," she said. "I'm sorry. It's my brother. I can't stop thinking about him."

Her brother, she told him, lived in a home for the mentally disabled. She cared for him once, but the state no longer allowed it. She didn't go into details and he didn't ask. He said things like "that's terrible" and "don't blame yourself" and she talked about how much she missed him and how she wished she could take care of him again. She said his name was Kenny and that he was good-natured and kind and that no one could understand him the way she could. She said it wasn't his fault he was hyper-sexual, and it wasn't fair that he was no longer allowed to live in the co-ed home. She said he'd go crazy.

"He grew up in a house with all sisters," she said. "He doesn't know how to live with those people."

All Steven could think about was an exit strategy, and a break in the story where he could make his move and leave.

"When he was eighteen, he used to take my mother's underwear and bring it to bed. Isn't that funny? I guess he liked feeling the fabric against his skin. He has needs, just like everyone else. He loves pretty girls. There's nothing wrong with that. He's loving, that's all."

*He loves pretty girls.*

An uneasiness settled in Steven's stomach. He remembered her ritual, cleaning him off, the baby talk, the singsong voice: *Here come all the pretty girls.*

He stood, stumbling over the coffee table.

"Where are you going?"

With lipstick smeared and eyeliner running down her face, she looked crazed, incestuous, neurotic …

Steven felt sick.

"I … I have to go," he stammered, walking to the door.

"You bastard!" She rose from the sofa. Her face twisted with rage and resembled a mad clown. "You think there's something *wrong* with me? You think I'm sick? You don't know. No one knows."

Steven lunged for the door.

There was a sound, a sudden *whack* coupled with an explosion of pain, a field of sparks and flickering lights, the sensation of stepping out of himself, and finally darkness.

Steven woke to the smell of rubber and gasoline and thought in a sudden panic that he had been in a car accident. His head was throbbing, although it wasn't quite pain, just a strange, sinking heaviness.

*I'm not in the street. I'm in a hospital bed.*

He tried to lift his arms, but they were secured.

*I must be incubated. I must have been pulling at the tube or something.*

The room was dark, but he wasn't blind. He saw soft gray shapes and shadows.

*I'm probably in an ICU. I'm probably banged up, but I can feel my legs. I can wiggle my toes, so I'm not paralyzed.*

As he formed these thoughts, they tumbled away from him like pieces of paper caught in a breeze.

*I must be on serious drugs.*

He was wearing some kind of mask with a hose attached to it, and could see it if he looked at his nose. He clenched his teeth to feel the breathing tube, but there was nothing there.

*What the fuck is that smell?*

But he knew it was gasoline.

*This isn't right.*

"Good, you're awake. I hope I didn't hurt you too much."

S.C. HAYDEN

And then she was standing over him.

He remembered his hand on the doorknob and the explosion of pain. She had hit him with something, knocked him out.

*That crazy bitch.*

Forgetting he was restrained, he tried lunging at her.

*She's got me tied to the fucking bed!*

His tongue was numb.

"I know you're afraid, but in time you won't be. I know what I'm doing. I've done my homework. It's going to be pleasant for you."

Understanding formed in his mind.

"The gas is going to fix your problems, and in a different way, it's going to fix mine. Every need you have will be taken care of. I'll feed you and wash you and, of course, I'll take care of this."

She cupped his testicles and flaccid penis.

His thoughts were like miniature clowns cartwheeling away, smiling and waving when he tried to grasp them.

*She has me tied down in bed and I'm breathing gasoline fumes through a mask. I'm high as a kite and I can't do anything about it.*

She stroked him with her hand.

The feeling was incredible.

Steven grew hard despite his fear, a disconnection between mind and body.

*Fuck no, fuck no, fuck no.*

He was hyperventilating and had to control his breathing.

*Slow down, slow down. Every breath is poison.*

How long before the fumes caused permanent damage? A few hours? What would happen after a day, a week, a month? Would he even know who he was after that long? Would he care?

"Don't worry, Kenny," she whispered softly, her voice swimming in his mind, reedy and hollow, a faint echo receding from the last syllable, "I'll take good care of you."

# With Rising Alarm

## Lawrence Conquest

The pregnant pause of an early winter morning breaks as an alarm clock wails like a crying baby. Rising from the calming depths, the hollow woman wakes. She rolls to the sound, thrusting an arm aloft from the enclosing bedding like a swimmer breaking the surface of a tranquil pool, her eyes still bound with sleep. She reaches blindly for the familiar contours of the rectangular box and hugs it to her chest.

The hollow woman scrunches her t-shirt about her neck and gently presses the swell of a naked breast against the rigid plastic of the clock radio. The alarm stills and soon the woman feels a familiar comforting pull as artificial lips pucker through the plastic grill and clamp about her nipple. The radio suckles like a leech. Breast milk passes through her body and into the clock. A thin overspill of the

159

watery white fluid patters onto the bed sheets.

Dimly, the woman senses the electrical heartbeat of light-emitting diodes as the clock counts down the seconds against her chest; a stable pulse, this fragile echo mingles with her own.

This clock projects in red.

It was a present from Jonathan. He'd bought it sometime before he left. You could wake up to radio or an alarm tone, according to the manual.

An alarm has been set this morning, but the woman can think of no good reason to rise. No *good* reason at all.


The only noise in the room is soft and wet.

The woman dozes.

The clock suckles.

Pallid light creeps through a crack in the curtains and stages a slow advance across the bed covers. All is calm. Until—

*Wa-ah!* the alarm cries, its plastic mouth encrusted with drying milk.

The woman shifts, lost in some internal fog, and presses her other breast close to the machine's impossible lips.

*Wa-ake up!* the alarm cries, unsatisfied.

Emerging from sleep, the woman catches her reflection in a bedside mirror. She is hollow inside. Thirty-four years old. Her eyes puffy from crying. Nicotine stains her fingers and her blonde hair is cut short in the pageboy style Jonathan always liked.

*Wake up, mummy!*

*Wake up, mummy!*
*Wake up, mummy!*

She may or may not be a mother.

Hush little one, she calls. Mummy is here, what do you want? Shall I bounce you on my knee?

*Wee-ee!* the clock coos. *Wee-ee! Wee-ee!*

Elsewhere upon the bedside cabinet, recumbent amongst the discarded bric-a-brac of pills and cigarettes, are a slew of books and leaflets. Words cropping up on the covers of these texts include *coping*, *dealing with*, and *surviving*. The longest of the words is *meningomyelocele*, though the woman prefers the term *spina bifida cystica*.

*Wake! Up!* the alarm cries.

The woman realizes she's been dreaming again. Something bright, melodic and moronic is playing on the clock radio, but the longer she listens the more she is convinced the words have somehow twisted out of true. Each chorus seems infected with repetition. The same word—over and over. Teasing her. Taunting her.

*Be my baby*, the radio sings. *Baby be good to me. Baby I love you. Baby I love only you.*

What's wrong, baby?

A hundred singers' voices merge into one howling discord.

Would you like mummy to sing you a song? Would you like mummy to sing you to sleep?

In the empty bedroom, the hollow woman croons a mournful lament for lost dreams and lost innocence.

After a while, the radio joins in.

The woman hides from the real world and the consequences of rising. Sleep seems the safest option, but no sooner does she feel a blissful negation of reality sweep over her when a jovial Irish voice intrudes.

*Wake Up To Wogan.*

She reaches for the snooze button, but after hearing her name read out on air, she hesitates.

*I believe we have a phone-in caller now*, declares the radio presenter. *What's your name, caller?*

*I don't have a name yet, do I, mummy?* The voice is lighter in tone, like a child's. *What is my name, mummy? Do I even get a name, mummy?*

"I don't know," mouths the woman. She utters no sound, but a delayed echo of her voice broadcasts from the radio. It sounds nothing like her.

I just don't know what to do. For the best.

The clock radio is silent for a while, as if thinking, until something outside the room disturbs it.

*Mummy, what's that noise?*

An electronic cry rises through the floorboards.

It's just mummy's phone. They're probably wondering why I haven't turned up for the appointment yet.

*Will you be going, mummy?*

I don't know. Can I break free of you? Should I even try? Shall I turn you off? Could I unplug you, even if I wanted to?

The woman gently tugs the power cable trailing from the alarm clock and a sharp pain shoots inside her belly. She traces the path of the cable as it snakes under the sheets. The alarm isn't plugged into the wall at all. A black plastic umbilical cord stretches out from between her legs to the inanimate object, which pulses with regular gushes of nourishing blood. The clock waits at the end of the rope like a curiously dislodged organ, her body the life-support keeping this most unnatural of infants alive.

The woman thinks of the bundle of skin and bone hovering between life and death in the sterile environment of the local hospital neonatal unit, and shudders.

I can't think about this now, she tells the clock. My head's not on straight. Will you let me rest? If I tell you a story, will you go back to sleep?

*Does the story have a happy ending, mummy? I like stories with happy endings.*

I know darling, that's why they are stories. Real life is more complicated.

*But how does my story end, mummy?*

If you want to know, baby, I'll tell you. Listen:

"The pregnant pause of an early winter morning breaks as an alarm clock wails like a crying baby. Rising from the calming depths, the hollow woman wakes ..."

# Newton's Third Law

### Frisco Macae

The pencil sat there.

That tiny insignificant piece of tree shaped by machine and filled with graphite had been more frustrating for Brian Boeing than the three months he had dated Becky Goldman, a girl in high school who refused to put out and then became a slut in college. After months of formulating, reading, and pretending he understood, Brian thought he had finally mastered psychokinesis.

The idea formed when he was sitting in physics and his professor said something about objects comprising of specks bouncing against each other. These specks never occupied a specific space, except for when they occupied all space. Brian researched various studies, journal entries, anything he could get his hands on. He discovered that electrons were waves of potential, which meant they were never in one specific place at any given time, but in all places, unless observed. Once under observation, electrons chose specific points in which to exist so the observer could see them.

Brian assumed humans could not grasp the idea that an object, such as a pencil, could be in all places and no place at once. It was this idea of human delusion that made him believe in psychokinesis. If all matter was made of particles, then nothing was truly solid, and if nothing was truly solid, then anything should be possible.

An anecdote was written on his mirror in red dry erase marker. He read it out loud every time he saw it: *humans are limited only in thought.*

"The problem is that we take everything at face value," Brian told the pencil. "We base our facts on how things appear, instead of the way they are."

He picked up the pencil and brought it to his eyes.

"You, my friend, are quite realistically less solid than water, so why is it you won't *move across this goddamned table!*"

He threw the pen and it ricocheted off the wall and onto the beer-stained carpet of his apartment.

"I don't get it."

Brian closed his eyes momentarily and reached for a thumbtack. He set it on his desk and placed a handmade paper windmill upon it. It teetered from side to side until it balanced. It spun clockwise for a few seconds and then changed directions.

He looked at the pencil intently and closed his

eyes. Nothing happened, so he retrieved it from the floor.

"I'm not even touching you," he informed the pencil. "We're bouncing protons back and forth. Sensory perception is simulation of what our brain assumes we should feel. My brain is assuming that holding you should feel like this, but it could be wrong."

Brian closed his eyes again.

"If all matter is made of tiny particles, then nothing is truly solid, and if nothing is solid, then anything should be possible."

He allowed one of his eyes to pry open.

The pencil rested on the flat of his palm.

"You're not even in my hand."

The clock on his computer informed him it was 1:34 in the morning.

"If our shared protons belong to me, then I can control them."

There was a warmth as the pencil floated above his palm. It stayed there for fractions of a second before falling and rolling to the floor.

His mouth was like a door cracked open to let in enough light to keep monsters at bay.

"Nothing is solid," he said to the empty room. "Nothing."

Brian slid his chair closer to the desk and wrapped three fingers around the cold wood. He breathed in deeply and the wood gave. It did not break away, but rather caved in like gelatinous mahogany. When his fingers dipped into the wood, he panicked.

"What the fuck!"

Brian pulled back, splintering the now solid desk. He screamed as skin ripped away from his fingertips and stayed behind in the wood. He reached for his cell with a set of bloody nubs and attempted to dial. Instead of pressing buttons, the phone melted against his finger. Flesh and bone dripped onto the carpet.

"Help!"

Brian leapt from his chair and reached his disfigured hand for the door to his apartment. The brass knob squeezed like modeling clay. He ripped the knob from the door and dropped it to the floor where it melted into the ground.

"No! Please help!"

The walls remained silent.

And then he sank.

Warmth surrounded his feet as he disappeared to his ankles in the floor.

Brian screamed until his voice cracked.

"Please," Brian said around sobs.

He was waist deep.

"This doesn't make sense."

There was nothing under him but the foundation. He raised his arms above his head as the ground reached his chest. Chest deep, Brian set both hands flat against the ground as if he were climbing out of a manhole. Instead of pushing himself to safety, his hands melted into the ground and disintegrated into flesh-colored gelatin.

"Newton's Third Law!" he said in a panic.

"'Mutual forces of action and reaction between two bodies are equal, opposite and collinear.' If I'm pushing against the ground, the ground's pushing against me!"

Brian pressed against the floor with the last of his strength. His hands did not melt into the floor and the ground did not give way, but he was unable to push himself out.

Weeping, he sank.

His mouth and nose dissolved into the ground and there was silence. A few tears dripped from his eyes, which disappeared into the floor.

The pencil rested on the carpet.

# The Truth Box

## David Jordan

Turning down a shadowy aisle at the Renaissance Faire, Lance Howard encountered a black tent with a sky-blue, rainbow-shaped sign arcing over its entrance. *Starrgazer's*. The jagged white letters resembled lightning.

"Hello, my friend," said a man behind a glass-topped counter. Tall and slender, he had white hair cascading past his shoulders and wore a flowing blue robe decorated with silver stars. "How might I be of assistance?"

Lance shrugged. He had an hour to kill before meeting Abby for lunch.

"Just looking."

"Look to your heart's content," said his host. "A man who doesn't look cannot see."

A large astrological chart hung on one wall. A mobile of stars and planets dangled from the roof in a corner. A rickety bookcase crammed with worn leather-bound volumes occupied another wall. Lance spotted a small wooden box the size in which cigars are customarily sold.

"How much is this?" Lance said, feeling the smooth cedar lid.

"You don't want that."

"I don't?" Lance lifted the hinged lid, exposing walls lined with blue velvet. He collected boxes, chests, cases, and interesting small containers of just about any kind. "Why not?" A white card the size and shape of a playing card, bearing a large black question mark, was at the bottom.

The robed man crossed to Lance's side and said, "These would serve you better." He held two metal balls adorned with spiky protuberances.

"What are they?"

"Magnets. They eliminate pain. Headache? Roll them over your forehead and the headache disappears. Same for a backache or stiff neck. They draw out pain from the body."

"I'm not much into new-agey stuff."

"They work. Guaranteed. Try them. Bring them back if they don't. Ezra Starr stands behind his wares."

"You're Ezra?"

"I am."

"I'm more interested in this box." Lance shifted the card at the bottom. "What's the card, though? It comes with the box?"

"You don't want that," Starr said again.

"That's not much of a sales pitch."

"Purchase the magnets. They will benefit you."

"The box won't?"

"That is not merely a box."

"What is it, then?"

"A device for obtaining truth."

"A truth box?"

"One could express it that way."

"How does it work? Like those plastic eight-balls?"

"The truth is not a toy."

Lance inspected the box more closely.

"How much?"

"Truth is without price, for those strong enough to accept it."

"The box," Lance insisted. "How much?"

Starr slipped the magnets into a pocket in his robe, studied him for a long moment. "A hundred dollars."

"That's a lot for such a small box." Lance rotated the thing in his hands.

"As I said, it is not merely a box."

"Yeah, it's a device for obtaining truth. How does it work?"

Starr took the box, opened the lid and gazed inside.

"Take an object that has come into intimate contact with the person you wish to question. Place it inside the box with the card bearing the question mark. At dusk, on a cloudless night, place the box outdoors under starlight. The next morning, present the box to that person and have them remove the card. While in possession, he or she must answer all questions with utmost truthfulness."

"Truth or dare, something like that?"

"The truth is not a game no more than it is a toy," Starr said, frowning. "It is not a trifling matter."

"A hundred bucks?"

"The price of the magnets is more reasonable," Starr said. "They would serve you well."

Lance liked the box. He could use it to stash his unruly collection of business cards. He currently stored them in a tattered envelope on top of the desk in his den and they spilled every time he looked for a pen or stamp.

"I'll buy the box," Lance said, pulling out his wallet.

Ezra Starr bowed slightly.

"As you wish, my friend."

"You bought something." Abby gestured toward the paper sack.

"Another box." Lance rolled his eyes. "Someday I'll find just the right one."

"Let's see."

He tilted the bag to show her the cedar lid.

"Very nice. A worthwhile addition to your vast collection."

"I suppose. Can't have too many boxes. How about you? Any luck on the drapes?"

"They had a nice yellow at Nagel's, but I'm not sure yellow would go with the wallpaper."

"You'll come up with something." Lance took his wife's hand. "You always do."

Lance noticed the question mark card on the floor of his den a few evenings later. He must have dropped it while placing the box on his desk. Wouldn't it be crazy if it worked? He could give it to Abby and find out why she married him, why she loved him, or learn about her life before they married, those old days she claimed "didn't matter." Maybe she would tell him how she lost her virginity. Abby had slept with other men before marrying him, but never talked about it. He tried to remember the rules of the card.

Lance glanced out the window. The evening sky stretched west to a deepening blue. Late June had brought a series of cloudless days. And starlit nights.

In their bedroom, he opened the top drawer of Abby's dresser.

What had come into more "intimate contact" than her panties? He placed a pair inside the box and took it outside, making sure no tree limbs or other obstacles obscured the sky where he balanced it atop the brick barbecue.

Lance rose at daybreak and crept outside to fetch the box, which glistened with dew as he carried it to the garage. He dried it with a rag, stashed it on a shelf behind a jug of antifreeze and headed out for the thirty-minute jog he had given as a reason for rising so early.

Interrogating Abby while their two daughters were home from school would be impossible. He needed a block of time when they could be alone, so he invented a fake eye exam and left work early.

"Hello, stranger," Abby said as he opened the kitchen door. "What brings you home so early?"

"An uncontrollable urge to see my lovely wife." He crossed to the sink where she was peeling potatoes, and took her in his arms.

She pecked him on the cheek. "Seriously, what's up?"

Lance shrugged. "I had some comp time coming from flogging Georgina Gibson's grammar text to deadline last month, so I took it."

"Are you hungry? I can make you a sandwich."

"Sure," Lance said, "I'll be right back."

He walked into the garage and retrieved the box from behind the antifreeze, removed the panties, dropped them in a laundry basket by the washer, and carried the box into the house.

"My wonderful wooden box." Lance said. "From the Renaissance Faire."

"Very nice. But what are you doing with it?"

Lance sat at the table and motioned for Abby to take a seat.

"I'll show you."

He slid the box halfway across the table and raised the lid to expose the card with the question mark.

"What am I missing here?" she asked.

Lance smiled. "Magic."

"Magic?" Abby's eyebrows arched skeptically.

"Anyone who reaches into the box and takes that card must give a truthful answer to all questions asked."

"You're kidding."

"Nope. The old guy who sold it to me guarantees it. Ezra Starr."

"You never mentioned anything when you bought it."

"I didn't think you would believe me." Lance dipped his head sheepishly. "You probably don't believe me now, but I'd like to try it anyway. Pick up the card."

"Pick it up?"

"Sure."

Abby shrugged, reached into the wooden box and removed the card.

"What do I do with it?"

"Just hold it. I'm going to ask you a series of questions."

"Ask away."

"What is your name?"

"Abigail Eileen Howard. It used to be Morris. Abby Morris, before I got married. You're wasting your questions."

"How much do you weigh?"

Abby flinched. She leaned back in her chair, sat in silence for a while and said, "One hundred forty-four pounds."

Fourteen pounds heavier than she habitually admitted, twenty more than what was listed on her driver's license.

"See?"

Abby bore a vague expression, as if her mind had traveled elsewhere.

"Who was the first boy you kissed?"

"Spencer Arns."

"How did you happen to kiss Spencer Arns?"

"He walked me home after school one day in seventh grade. It was April. He grabbed me as we went through the railroad underpass on Revere Street."

"Did you enjoy it?"

"Sort of. He wore braces, so it kind of hurt. Weird more than painful. He was a funny guy, but not very cute. He made a lot of jokes."

Lance drew in a deep breath.

"How did you lose your virginity?"

"I went ice skating with Casey Belloti and a few of our friends. We went out and goofed around. It was lots of fun. Gwen was with us but she wouldn't skate. We had two cars and when we started home, I rode with Casey. On the way to town, Casey turned off on a Forest Service road and parked in the snow. He kissed me. I kissed him back. He put his hand under my sweater, on my breast. The windows fogged. I was in the front seat with my sweater up and my jeans down. Casey took off his pants but left his shirt on because of the cold. It didn't hurt much. People said it would, but it didn't."

"My god," Lance whispered.

Casey Bellotti was the husband of Abby's oldest sister, Gwen. He and Gwen, married twenty years, had three sons.

"When did this happen?" Lance asked.

"My senior year of high school. I was seventeen."

Gwen and Casey had been married barely a year then, and had no children. Casey was six years older than Abby.

"What happened between you and Casey after that?"

"He said he loved me and that we'd go away together after I finished school. We sneaked around. I'd tell my parents I was going to a movie and meet him at a motel. He didn't care about Gwen, but then she got pregnant. He said it wouldn't be right to desert a pregnant wife. So we didn't leave."

"Did you still sneak around?"

"Twice after Gwen got pregnant. I didn't like it. He wanted to keep doing it, but I felt bad. He said maybe when the baby got older he could leave her, but I thought everything had gotten too creepy, us hiding in motel rooms while my sister was sitting at home with a kid growing inside her."

"You were jealous?"

"It was weird. But jealous, too, I guess. He said they didn't get along. They had to be doing more than arguing, though, if it made her pregnant. He said he loved me, but having sex with Gwen was a strange way of showing it."

"You stopped seeing him?"

"I finished high school, took a summer job at a resort in California. Two hundred miles from home and from Casey. I started college that fall, even farther away. I went home for holidays and stayed for only as long as I had to. He always followed me around, whispering to me in the family room while the folks set the table for Thanksgiving dinner, grabbing me under mistletoe at Christmastime. By the time I finished college, he and Gwen had another baby."

"Does he still do that sort of thing ... try to kiss you at Christmas?"

Lance had never cared much for Casey, but he assumed it was merely a matter of mismatched temperaments, book editor vs. car salesman, introvert vs. extrovert. When Casey pontificated about investing in wheat options or launched into slight-of-hand tricks like pulling nickels from the ears of nephews and nieces, Lance left the room. It never occurred to him that while he thumbed through magazines in the den, Casey might be kissing his wife.

"Last Christmas Eve," Abby said, "he followed me into the bathroom. First thing he tried in years. He kissed me. Groped my rear. I just looked at him. Elbowed his hands off."

"You didn't tell him to stop?"

"He got the message."

"Are you in love with him?"

"No."

"But you were?'

"When I was seventeen."

"You got over it?"

"Eventually. I drank."

During all their years together, Abby was a tee-totaler. When other people drank beer, she drank soda. She told him she tried drinking when she was younger, but it made her sick.

"When?"

"After I found out Gwen was pregnant. I would start feeling bad, so I'd drink to turn off the bad feeling. I drank until I didn't feel much of anything. I kept it up for a long time. I'm not proud."

They sat in silence for a moment. He searched her eyes; they had drifted.

"Were there other guys after Casey? Before me?"

"Yes."

"How many?"

"I don't know."

It was an evasive answer. Was the effect of the card wearing off, or did it sometimes falter? Could the person holding it conceal thoughts?

"Why don't you know?"

"I drank a lot."

"So much that you don't remember?

"I don't try to remember, really."

"These are guys you slept with? Had sex with?"

"I suppose."

"You suppose? You don't know?"

"There were a lot of guys. parties, taverns,.and bars. I drank until I stopped feeling bad. Sometimes things happened. I'd wake in my bed with the pillow smelling like English Leather, but nobody around. I'd wake at someone else's apartment and it would be empty. There were times I didn't know if I'd had sex. I couldn't tell. I'd wake half-dressed on some couch with a terrible headache."

"I can't believe it."

Abby didn't respond.

"What guys can you remember?"

Abby frowned and narrowed her eyes as if peering down a dark corridor in search of a lighted doorway.

"Aaron Elder," she said. "Spring of senior year. We'd park behind the sawmill east of town, lay the back seats flat and spread the blanket in the luggage compartment. Randy Davis. We worked together in Sonora. He was older, twenty-one. We fooled around one night and I woke up in his bunk. It happened two or three times. He wrote me letters in the fall, but I never answered them. Larry Ross. I wound up in his bed one morning. He had a duplex. Mike Nehl. He played baseball. Bill Workman. He was a TA in my Civ class. Sid. The guy who flipped burgers at Beef-a-Rama. He came to a party at a friend's house. A couple guys ... I don't remember their names."

Lance shook his head. "A wild child, weren't you?"

"Unhappy child," she said. "It wasn't much fun, really."

"Who else?"

"Keith Greene. He worked for my dad. I had

this huge crush on him, but he had no interest in me. He thought of me as his boss's kid. He lived in this one-room house over by Papandrea's Pizza. I'd take my mom's car and drive past, hoping he'd notice and ask me in. One night around eleven o'clock, I knocked on his door. I'd been drinking and I more or less dragged him into bed."

"So that's what, seven that you remember?"

"I never counted."

"And the two you forgot, or didn't know."

"I sometimes have trouble remembering."

"There were others?"

Abby nodded.

"Gary Toberg. Scott Silverman. Rod Mrozinksi."

"Okay," Lance said. "That's enough."

"Ken Taylor. Fall of sophomore year. He lived in the apartment next door. Al Nichols from my psych class. Jake Johnson in the hot tub at the lake—"

"That's *enough!* I don't want to hear it."

"Wade Fulton ..."

Lance snatched the card from Abby's hands.

She shook her head and smiled. "Well? Go ahead and ask."

Lance stared at her wordlessly.

"Questions," she said. "I'm ready. Fire away."

"It doesn't work," Lance murmured. He jammed the card into the box. "I knew it wouldn't work."

"You didn't ask anything. How do you know it doesn't work?"

"I asked your name. You just looked at me. I

asked how much you weighed."

"What did I say?"

"Nothing. Like I said, it doesn't work."

"I don't remember any questions. None at all."

"I guess you didn't listen closely. Don't worry about it. It's just a silly game."

Lance ducked into the bathroom and locked the door.

"My god," he said to the reflection in the mirror. His face had gone pale. Sweat beaded his upper lip. "Casey Bellotti?" All those Christmas Eves around the tree at his in-laws' with the Bellotti kids and the Howard girls and all the other cousins giggling and the gift paper rustling and the ribbons flying.

He counted the names with his fingers:

Bellotti, Keith Greene, Aaron Elder, Ken Taylor, Wade Fulton … fourteen, no, fifteen. Plus himself. Sixteen. And he had cut her short. She'd had at least three years to go in her premarital escapades. Lance suddenly had more information than he had bargained for. It would litter his mind forever.

While Abby gardened in the backyard the next morning, Lance drove to the Renaissance Faire. He found Ezra Starr behind the glass-topped counter in his black tent.

"I bought this here."

Lance placed the box on the counter.

"I recall you, my friend," Starr replied, "and I recall your purchase."

"I'd like to return it."

"The box did not work?"

Starr cocked an eyebrow.

"I didn't say that, but I don't want it anymore."

"You don't want the box, or you don't want the truth? The truth is not a game or a toy. I warned you. It is a force—a natural force like the wind. Unleashed, it can be brutal."

"Just take the box. You can keep the money."

"Once used, the box cannot be returned, any more than truth can be returned," Starr said. "It is yours forever."

"I don't want it," Lance said.

"I am sorry, my friend." Starr stepped around the counter. He swept the box off the glass, thrust it into Lance's arms and steered him by the elbow to the door. "The truth ... you must live with it."

Lance stumbled outside into the shadows.

# Always With Me

## Cynthia Witherspoon

I brushed my fingers across Sharon's cheek as it cooled from the summer heat. She was beautiful. Pretty as a picture. Still mine, despite her attempts to leave.

"You're too clingy, Stephen," she said before she had pulled away. "I can't breathe. I can't take *one* step without you."

I had to do it. I didn't have a choice. The bitch left me and took the girls. I couldn't be alone. I'd told her time and time again that I wouldn't be alone. The very thought left me breathless. They were my family, my everything.

I tried reasoning with her, tried explaining her importance to me, but she wouldn't listen. I heard my teeth grind.

*No, she never listened.*

I brushed stray hairs that had fallen over Sharon's

face and moved her hand around Tiffany. She and
Cassie were small and fragile like their mother. It
was a trait that rang too much with truth. Cassie sat
still, her dark eyes connecting to mine. She knew
how to behave and not to fidget while Daddy took
her picture. She was always the good one.

"Just relax. Smile. We're a family."

I laughed as I lifted the camera, snapping photograph after photograph of them posed just so. The
pictures were darling; they would never leave me.

I pulled out the laptop and grinned as the images
loaded onto the screen, each of my girls as pretty as
they had ever been in life. I saved the one I wanted,
deleted the rest, and kissed Sharon.

"Now we will always be together."

The photograph print was perfect. Late afternoon
sunlight had filtered through the curtains to create
haloes around their heads. Sharon had died with
her eyes open, that cold look she often gave me
now replaced by the gleam of reflected light. The
girls were adorable in their poses, holding onto
their mother as they rested on the couch.

My hands shook as I took out the album, my
*Book of the Dead*, which I had started long before
they entered my life. I flipped through the pages:
my mother in her coffin; my first love, Elizabeth,
propped against the chair she always sat in when
she came to my dorm room … she was the first;
twenty years had passed and she was still with me.
And the others, each posing for their final pictures

with grace only death can provide.

    I loved them all.

    I was eager to add my latest to the collection.

    There was no need for labels. I knew them all. Remembered when they were taken.

    They would never threaten to leave me alone.

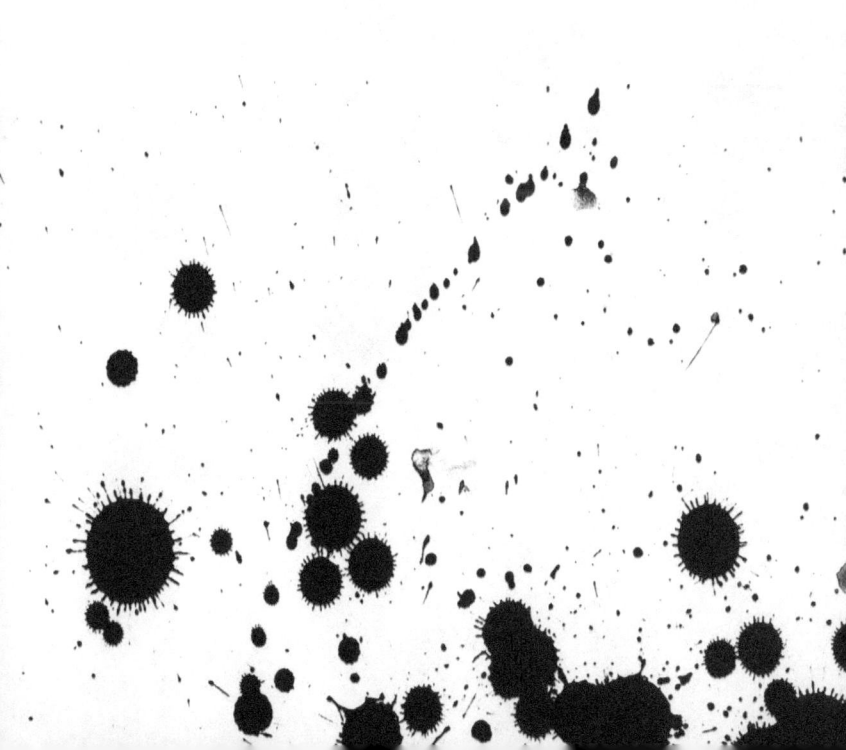

# Broken Reflections

### Amanda Pillar

Veronica Cameron smiled at her reflection and smoothed a few wispy strands of raven hair into place. Weak, early morning sunlight filtered into the bathroom, giving her skin a soft glow. She ran her hands over her Gucci suit. As of today, she was the assistant to the CEO at one of the biggest companies in Glasgow. Who would have thought?

*Certainly not my family.*

Veronica winced. But she was realistic, and the thought was true. Her parents loved her; there was no doubt about it. But they thought she was nothing more than a pretty face. Her dad used to tease her, saying that while her beauty could launch a thousand ships, her brain would sink them as there was no lighthouse to guide their journey.

*Just because I'm not the scientist he is.*

Taking a deep breath, she shoved the thoughts

aside; they would do her no good; and she should be reveling in her newly won supremacy.

Turning back, she saw there was a dark smudge in one corner of the chrome-framed mirror. Frowning, she tried to wipe the surface clean with a bath towel. The mark wouldn't budge.

"That's odd," she muttered.

Realizing she'd be late if she didn't hurry, she cast one last glance at the mirror, grabbed her handbag and rushed out the door.

*Veronica's Journal, February 10th 2009*

*For once in my life, things seem to be going well. In fact, everything is fantastic! I love my job and my boss, and I have made fantastic new friends. I love knowing Dad feels ashamed of himself, and how he's talked to me all these years.*

*But I can't help feeling that something isn't quite right.*

*I'm seeing things in the mirror. Not every time, but enough that I've started to notice it ... the dark smudge in one corner. At first, I thought it was dirt, and I kept trying to wipe it clean. I thought the mirror was scratched, so I replaced it ... but now I don't. I think it's another person, far in the distance, which is crazy, because whenever I turn around, no one's there.*

Veronica sat in the cushiony chair in her optometrist's office and gave a rather shaky grin. Dr. Gordan was a nice man, with a shock of white hair and bright blue eyes. He pulled his little swivel chair closer and smiled as he sat.

"Veronica, how can I help you today?" His voice was deep, soothing.

"I was hoping for a check-up."

She was too nervous to ask if he could test her to see if she had a blind spot in one eye, or if something was wrong and that's why she was seeing things.

*He'll find something, if there's something to find.*

"Your last appointment was six months ago. Your eyes were perfect then."

Veronica forced another smile.

"I recently started a new job, and I have been getting headaches."

This was mostly true; although her job wasn't giving her headaches, far from it. She loved every minute she spent pandering to the CEO's whims. She was needed. Her boss told her at least a thousand times a day how fantastic she was. So it wasn't work.

*But seeing things in mirrors would hurt anyone's brain.*

"Okay, we'll start with the basics."

*Veronica's Journal, February 22nd 2009*

*Dr. Gordan said there's nothing wrong with my eyes. But I don't understand that …*

*something is going on.*

*I've been paying attention to the smudge in the mirror (all the mirrors in my house)—it's there all the time now—and the outline is clear. It's a woman. But I can't see her face; it's too fuzzy. I can't brush my teeth, put my make-up on or do my hair without seeing her there; it's distracting.*

*I keep telling myself she isn't real ... but I don't believe myself half the time.*

*What's wrong with me?*

Veronica dropped her leg from the bathroom basin and rinsed out the face washer. She wiped the soap from her freshly shaven leg and rinsed the peach colored material again.

In a few hours, she would be out on a date, her first one in a month. Butterflies danced in her stomach, and she couldn't keep the silly grin from her face.

She'd met her date at a work dinner. His name was David Martin and he was highly respected in the stock market world. He was reportedly worth millions, which was nice. But what she liked most about him was that he thought she was beautiful and smart.

Her dark eyebrows surged together when she noticed a splash of blood on the surface of the mirror. How had she managed to flick it there? She didn't remember cutting herself while shaving.

Veronica grabbed the face washer and rubbed at

the blood. Rinsing the cloth, she realized that the mark was still there. Her stomach turned to stone and sank to the floor.

Blindly, she reached out to the window, jerking the blinds wide, hoping the bright sunlight would burn the image away. It didn't.

*It's her.*

Veronica's skin tingled. She stared at her cell phone, wondering if she should cancel the date. Her head was pounding. She felt sick.

The woman's hair was the color of blood.

*Veronica's Journal, March 16th 2009*

*I can't believe this. I can't. I mean, you don't see people in the mirror that aren't there, do you?*

*I saw her face. I've tried and tried to think of a way to describe it, but nothing does it justice. It's angular and she has eyes like blue crystal, a wide mouth and a strong nose. Like someone out of the past with her hair done up and her gown centuries out of date.*

*I keep being drawn to her cold, empty eyes. Aren't eyes meant to be the window to the soul?*

Veronica pinned her hair into a ponytail as she readied for her morning jog. It was Sunday; she had the whole day ahead of her and David wanted to have dinner with her tonight.

This was going to be their fourth date. She was hoping to take it to the next level and she wanted to appear fit.

Pulling on a white headband, she grinned at her reflection, eyes automatically avoiding the woman in the mirror.

"I look *good* for a run," she said, excited.

She wanted this to work with David. It would prove to her mother and father how far she'd come.

Feeling happier than she had in a while, she decided it was time to face the woman in the mirror.

Veronica knew she wasn't real, knew something in her brain was going on, but she couldn't bring herself to see a doctor. They might think she was crazy, and she wasn't. She was as sane as anyone else.

"You aren't real," she said to the image.

The woman turned. A dart of electricity surged Veronica's spine as blue crystal eyes bore into her, seeing through her. The room was freezing. Her breath puffed into mist as it emerged from her lips.

*She hates me.*

It was the only way she could describe the look on her face.

*Veronica's Journal, May 31st 2009*

*I've been thinking about this journal a lot lately, even though I've avoided writing in it. I thought that if I stopped, maybe the woman would go away, that by writing it all down, I was giving it—her—a kind of permanence.*

*I was being an idiot.*

*I don't see my reflection anymore. I haven't seen it for a while. Whenever I look in a mirror, it's her that's there. She hasn't looked at me though, not since that first time. I take it as a small favor.*

*Mom and Dad think there's something wrong with me. They keep asking about my health, more than they ever did before, and they call all the time to check on me. It could be because I look strange, I don't know. David hasn't said anything though, so I don't think it's that.*

*Although, it is hard to know what you look like when you can't see your reflection; for all I know, I could've grown a mole or a beard. Okay, I'm exaggerating. No signs of a beard, thank heavens for that. I don't think beards are all that wonderful on women and I'm sure David would have said something about that!*

*How did I get off topic? I keep doing that, losing my train of thought.*

*What's wrong with me?*

*I'm not crazy, am I?*

Veronica rolled over in bed, her mind dragged from the depths of sleep by the sound of humming. Opening her eyes to silvery coated darkness, she turned onto her back and then slowly sat upright, the duvet falling away from her.

The night air was cool as it came in through the curtain-less window.

She listened for the sound of a human voice. It was silent.

Reaching the far corner of her room, her eyes stopped on a shadowed area.

Veronica's heart pounded as she saw grey cloth reflecting the moonlight and a pale oval shape.

*A face.*

Her heart slammed into her ribs and her breathing hastened.

She was going to faint.

"Who's there?"

No one answered.

Scrabbling for her bedside lamp, she switched it on. A soft glow fell across the empty room.

Stepping out of the shower, Veronica wrapped a peach-colored towel around her body, nearly crying, but she'd done enough of that in the last few days. Her throat was sore, and her eyes puffy.

David had broken up with her.

It was hard to believe; he'd seemed so interested. Everything had been great; everything. They'd been able to talk, to laugh, and the sex had been fantastic.

*But he thought I was cheating on him.*

It hurt deeply that he'd even suspected she could do something like that. But he'd known she was hiding something from him, and she couldn't tell him what it was when he asked.

How could he understand about the woman in the mirror? The woman who wasn't real. The woman whose very presence meant that Veronica was going crazy, if she wasn't already.

Turning to the mirror, Veronica's eyes widened with surprise.

The woman was gone.

There was no tell-tale flash of grey or red.

"Don't tell me I had to break up with David to get you to disappear," she said.

It wouldn't be fair.

No movement came from the mirror, and so she walked up to it. She hadn't seen her face in ages. Veronica nearly didn't recognize her reflection. Her cheeks were hollow and there were dark shadows under her eyes.

*I look haunted.*

It wasn't surprising that David had known she was keeping something from him.

About to hang her towel on the rack, her arm stopped mid-motion and she stared at the shower. There was writing on the misted screen.

Her neck cracked as she whipped around, searching for the woman.

No one was there.

Turning back to the mirror, she saw that along with her reflection was the writing on the screen: "Nothing lasts forever."

*Veronica's Journal, June 3 2009*

*I'm starting to crack. I can feel it. I wish I couldn't see this woman, I do. She's everywhere I go: in windows, surfaces, mirrors ...*
  *Why won't she leave me alone?*
  *I don't want to be crazy.*
  *I don't.*

Veronica smashed every mirror in her house but one. She left the bathroom mirror alone. It was a warning.

She'd been fired from her dream job. The job she'd loved and had worked so hard to get. It was ridiculous. Unfair! It was more than unfair. The woman was trying to ruin her life; she had to be. What else had she meant by her message on the shower screen?

Sobbing in a pile of broken glass, Veronica froze.

Maybe it was her. Maybe she wanted herself to fail and her mind was sabotaging her. There was something wrong with her. There had to be.

She wanted to die. Simply die.

How was she going to explain this to her parents? They'd tell her that she shouldn't worry; an easier job would come along ...

She picked up a piece of mirror—one with the woman looking back at her—and then clamped it in her fist, ignoring the pain and the blood.

*Veronica's Journal, July 1 2009*

*Found a new job. It's nowhere near as good as my old one. I have to travel over forty minutes to work every day; it's in Edinburgh!*

*There was another message left for me. This time it was written on a piece of paper next to my bed.*

*"Hate consumes."*

*...*

*Just went to find the note, but I can't see it anywhere.*

*The handwriting was similar to my own.*

Veronica didn't drive often; she'd driven even less since the woman began to appear. She never blocked her view in the mirrors, but she was there, a little distraction Veronica didn't need on the busy roads.

She was traveling down the highway; she didn't have a destination in mind, just somewhere away from home. The afternoon traffic was heavy, which meant she had to concentrate. She liked that; it took her mind off ... *her.*

Something grey flashed in the corner of her vision. The woman was there, right there, sitting next to her in the passenger seat.

Her skin was white with a blue tinge, as if she'd drowned, and her-blood red hair hung down the sides of her face. Those empty, crystal-colored eyes stared into Veronica's and she panicked.

*You aren't paying attention.*

Veronica's car smashed into the back of an SUV at sixty miles per hour.

Everything went black.

Veronica sat on the couch at her parents' house, flicking channels on the TV remote. She'd broken her leg and a couple of ribs, so she was in nearly constant pain. A plaid rug was wrapped around her with her foot propped on a brown ottoman.

Someone walked into the lounge, and Veronica glanced up, thinking it was her mother. She shut her eyes and opened them again. The woman was sitting opposite her on the arm chair.

She hadn't seen her since the car accident.

Her mother entered and said, "Honey, what's wrong?"

"Can you see her?"

"Who?" Her mother stopped walking and stood in the center of the lounge, frowning.

Veronica nodded at the chair.

"She's sitting opposite me."

"Honey, you did suffer a head injury in the crash. Are you sure you're not seeing something? What do they look like?"

The woman stared at her blankly.

"She's not very tall, maybe five-foot-one. She has dark red hair, blue eyes, and is wearing a grey dress. Her skin has a blue tinge."

She remembered the latter from the car accident; it made her shiver.

Veronica didn't bother to describe the dress to her mother; it would make her sound even crazier. It was the most startling thing about the woman—after the hair—and it looked like a period costume, like something from a Jane Austen play. It was dull grey with embroidery all over the skirt. The dress didn't have a waist, and was gathered under the woman's breasts.

Her mother was silent for a long time. "What's her name?"

"I don't know."

*Call me Enid.*

She'd never remembered the quality of the woman's voice before. It was like wind murmuring through trees in a vacant forest—cold, earthy, whispery.

The hair on the nape of her neck and arms rose.

Her mother shook her. "Honey, what is it? Are you okay?"

"She says her name is Enid."

"Oh Honey, how long have you been seeing her? She's not real, baby, she's not there." Her mother was crying, great streams of tears.

Veronica pointed at Enid. "She's right there, I swear it."

But Enid was gone.

Veronica had been visiting Dr. McDougal for a month, and had been in and out of his clinic too many times to count. She'd even gone to the Southern General Hospital and had a MRI scan.

The doctor cleared his throat and glanced at his paperwork. "You don't have a brain tumor, which is the good news."

Veronica nodded, not relieved. If she'd had a tumor, it could have been removed and she'd return to normal. She could try and catch up with David again; she could live a normal life.

"But I do have bad news," Dr. McDougal said, a little sad.

"Why doesn't that surprise me?" she muttered.

"Sorry?"

Veronica shook her head. "Don't worry. What's the bad news?" She had wanted it to be a tumor.

The handsome psychiatrist bent forward, catching her eyes. "You have schizophrenia."

Her whole body felt like it had been slammed between two heavy pieces of machinery. Again.

Veronica held the XL-sized dress and fought tears. She'd been so small before the medication; fit and toned. The weight had piled on. Guys used to stare at her in the street.

*Funny how I used to wish people would look at my mind, rather than the outside.*

It was a terrible time to discover she was vain.

It was an ugly dress as well, but there wasn't a lot of choice in the store, and she was too embarrassed by her appearance to do her shopping in Glasgow. She might bump into somebody she knew. It was bad enough having to go to work looking like this; she didn't know how she'd handle seeing someone like David.

Veronica put the dress on the rack and calmly walked out of the store. She climbed into her car and leaned her head against the steering wheel, fighting for a slither of control. Enid was in the rearview mirror.

*I fucking hate my life.*

*Veronica's Journal, October 10th 2009*

> *Dr. McDougal says the meds need to be upped, that the dose is wrong. He also put me on antidepressants because I seem to be a little moody. Wouldn't you be moody if you looked more like a fat cow than a person?*
>
> *I'm starting not to care anymore. If the drugs aren't working, then what can I do?*
>
> *Is there any point?*

Veronica stood in the lounge room of her apartment. She'd been asked out to lunch, but she didn't want to go—didn't want to risk being seen by anyone. A sound from the bathroom turned her around. The shampoo or conditioner bottle could have fallen from the shower ledge. Walking into the room, she nearly tripped over her feet.

Enid was there ... holding Veronica's razor.

*Oh my god, she wants to kill me.*

Something inside her snapped.

*"GET OUT!"*

Veronica couldn't remember much after that,

but when she realized Enid had finally left, piles of knickknacks lay smashed on the bathroom tiles. She must have thrown them.

A knock sounded on her door. Wearily, and with her hands bleeding from gripping broken porcelain, she answered it and faced a concerned neighbor.

*Veronica's Journal, October 15th 2009*

*I'm so tired.*

*I woke the other day with Enid standing over me. I think I caught her in the act of trying to kill me, I don't know.*

*The sad thing is … I don't care anymore. She can murder me if she wants. I'm okay with that. I'm sick of living, of being looked at like I'm some nutcase.*

*I wonder if a figment of my imagination can kill me. You're meant to die for real if you die in your dreams, right?*

*Even Mom and Dad are careful around me, as if they're mourning, like I've been long buried.*

*Maybe it would help if I disappeared.*

Feeling melancholy, Veronica popped a piece of chocolate into her mouth. There was no point in watching her weight. She ballooned out just from *looking* at food.

Her mother was on the phone in the other room.

"Clarice, I can't talk for long, Veronica's here."

A pause.

Her mother was talking to Veronica's aunt. "It's terrible. She's paranoid. I get worried she might do something to hurt someone, she swears this Enid person is still around, but, of course, no one else can see her."

Another pause.

"Her medication can't be upped anymore; they are already as high as they can be."

Veronica stopped listening.

Her mother thought she was a danger to other people.

Looking down at the half-eaten chocolate, she felt sick.

*Veronica's Journal, November 12<sup>th</sup> 2009*

*I've had enough. I'm so tired. I can't take it anymore.*

*I've taken a heap of painkillers. I already feel woozy. I'm going to slash my wrists. I want to make sure no one can revive me. I'm just—I can't—it's too much!*

*I'm sorry, Mom and Dad, I am. I didn't want to be a freak, and I tried. I did. The medication doesn't work. I can't pretend to be normal anymore.*

*I want to rest, to be free.*

*Please, Enid, leave me alone.*

A leather-bound diary and a large piece of glass lay next to a body, which was slumped in the bathtub, framed by the red rays of dying sunlight. All three were coated in blood. The glass shard wobbled slightly, vibrating. Within moments, a hand reached out from the mirror, the fingers bending to touch the surface.

A woman stepped out of the silvery fragment. Her blood-red hair swung around her as she walked toward Veronica. She sat on the edge of the bathtub, ignoring the tiny shards of glass pricking into her cold flesh. Crimson liquid was splashed everywhere and soon her grey gown was covered in the sticky, warm fluid.

Reaching a shaking hand forward, the woman searched for a pulse, her arm stilling as she met cool skin and a faint heartbeat. She ignored the diary and grasped Veronica's hand. A single, crystalline tear spilled from her eye and dropped onto the cooling limb.

Alone.

Again.

Enid watched as the last traces of life fled from her only companion, and reverently, she gathered them into herself.

*Also by Written Backwards*

*Anthologies*

PELLUCID LUNACY
CHIRAL MAD
CHIRAL MAD 2
QUALIA NOUS
THE LIBRARY OF THE DEAD
CHIRAL MAD 3
ADAM'S LADDER

*Attevon*

AT THE LAZY K
LIARS, FAKERS, AND THE DEAD WHO EAT THEM

*Collections*

BONES ARE MADE TO BE BROKEN
YES TRESPASSING